NOWHERE
TO GO BUT
MARS

D.H. Aire
a novella

Works by D.H. Aire

The Highmage's Plight Series
Highmage's Plight
Merchants and Mages
Human Mage
Highmage
Well Armed Brides
Prophecies Pawns
Paradox Lost

Hands of the Highmage Series
For Whom the Bell Trolls
Of Elves and Unicorns
Goldilocks and the Three Dwarves
Sleeping Beauties and Beasts

Dare2Believe Series
Dare 2 Believe
Double Dare
Triple Dare
Double Double* (forthcoming)

Terran Catalyst Series
Terran Catalyst
Plymouth Meets Rock

Other Works
Crossroads of Sin and Other Stories
Knight of the Broken Table
Lessers Not Losers

D.H. Aire

Nowhere to Go But Mars
has previously appeared in short story form
in the following anthologies:

Irony of Survival
(The Zharmae Publication Press, 2013)

and

Alternate Facts: Digital Science Fiction
(Digital Short Stories Anthology Series 3, Book 1, 2018).

Dedication

To Sarah

Acknowledgements

6

I gratefully thank my copyeditor, Karen MacLeod, for assistance in offering editorial advice on this book. Additionally, I wish to express my appreciation to Heidi Sutherlin for a wonderful cover design. As ever, I also wish to thank my family and friends for all their support.

Finally, to you, my friends and readers, who have purchased this book. Thank you for allowing this story to touch your lives.

Thank you.

D.H. Aire
January 2020

Table of Contents

Part One: Mars or Bust
Chapter 1 – Nowhere to Go But Mars

My life was toast. So, what the hell, I boarded the train and joined the millions of people on the trek to Death Valley, home of the Colonial Émigré Center.

"Proceed along the orange lines!" the rep ordered. "We're processing over three hundred thousand of you Colonial wannabees this week!"

"And they're only accepting fifty thousand of us this round," muttered the guy behind me.

I glanced at my new pal, Rafe, one of the many guys I'd made friends with in the last week or so. Apparently, Colonial Management was rather discriminating, and we Americans weren't considered the healthiest lot.

Those who could afford better weren't about to give up the cushy life for the less than palatial digs of the cave warrens of Mars. It would take generations of backbreaking work to terraform the planet, as well as house and feed a growing colony.

Voices in English, Spanish, even Spanglish, directed us to place our hands in the bio readers, scan the ID codes on our right forearms, check our baggage, and line up for the security check. "Men on the right. Women on the left."

I shook my head, glancing about me at the "men and women." I kept my mouth shut and joined the herd going through security and all the scanning equipment. Once on the other side of the security curtains, we were ordered to strip. I hesitated, and was told to drop the sweaty clothes I'd worn for days down the incinerator chute. I, and hundreds of others, briefly protested. The nearest guard muttered, "You can always leave, kid."

Yeah, right, I thought. I'd lived in the tent city out

there for over a week—and slept in line since the middle of the night just waiting for the Center to open. Even doing that, I was behind tens of thousands of people who had the same idea.

I tossed my clothes down the disposal chute without further protest and sniffed the air. My new friends and I stank worse than when we were huddled outside.

I continued down the line through processing, where the indignities didn't end. I gritted my teeth as they shaved off my hair, which was blown into vacuum vents built into the floor.

I'll say this for them, they certainly believed in cleanliness.

"You look stellar," Rafe muttered.

"Gee, you're one to talk," I replied.

He grinned. We were ushered to the line on the right. I was urged down the center lane. In that moment I knew that we'd likely never see each other again and, a moment later, our lines diverged and I lost sight of him.

A recorded voice ordered, "Place your hand on the bio reader… Do not move." I heard a click and saw a small square card on a cord drop out of the dispenser. "Please take your new biometric card. Slip the cord over your head… Note your number. Memorize it!"

A moment later, the recorded voice ordered, "Proceed along the orange line."

The President's speech changed the bleak prospects of our lives forever when she announced the deal the government made with the United Nations and Colonial Management.

The commentators called it: *"A challenge as great as John F. Kennedy's vision of an American walking on the Moon."*

The President said, *"Our country's at a crossroads. Our nation provides cheap labor to world powers like Australia, Afghanistan, Congo, and Korea, who were among the first to plant colonies on Mars… We've learned a lot from their mistakes, which cost tens of thousands of people their lives in the crossing. We have dramatically improved the odds of survival by knowing what we do now… That our young people have the best chance of surviving in hibernation—and it is so many of them, who have no prospects of a job and are living on the streets of our cities and towns, who also may see this as the opportunity it is… One that can offer them a new chance and can help humanity not just settle Mars, but one day take us out of the Solar System, altogether, to spread humanity across the galaxy."*

So, here I was, one of those young people— unskilled, homeless, but hopefully still healthy enough—I hoped—among colonial wannabees, who lined up to leave the huddled masses of America for the Land of Opportunity, Mars.

"Name," the Colonial Management official said.

"Gary Grime," I replied, shivering under the blast of air conditioning as I covered my privates.

"Age?"

"Fifteen."

"Marital status?"

"Single."

"Do you have plans to marry before the launch?"

"No, Sir."

"Your preference, then."

"I'm hetro."

"Any money?"

"None," I said, having spent every last credit.

"Anything to declare?"

"No, Sir."

"No contraband in your belongings?"

"No, Sir," I asserted, knowing I was breaking no laws even if they might think my choice of items a bit odd.

"Then, that only leaves your picking a spouse based on compatibility parameters."

"I, uh, understand." I did; the only way to

efficiently cross space was to pack starships with hibernating colonists. The bitter reality—thousands of people still died in hibernation.

Though, it turned out that age was a key factor to surviving the trip was that those between twelve and twenty had the highest survival rates. But there was an ironic caveat to the age factor—those who hibernated in pairs, what the scientists referred to as keeping each other warm, had a ninety percent survival rate. Otherwise, hibernation was a practically a death sentence. The Net suggested this was likely linked to some mammalian survival instinct buried in our DNA.

All I knew is that I had a chance for a new life. Anything was better than living in the Hell I'd been.

The official said, "I must offer you one last opportunity to back out, Mr. Grime. It says here you completed your High School education in only three years," he tapped the computer tablet. "What's more impressive, it says you've even taken courses for college credit. So you understand the decision you've made. However, I must warn you, it's possible your spouse may be as young as twelve."

"Uh, yes, sir. I realize that." The irony didn't escape me. The effort to stave off rising teen pregnancy rates was meaningless for colonists. Colonial Management wanted us to breed like rabbits—as long as we left Earth.

The final irony of the whole damned thing was that the official considered my education impressive. It certainly hadn't helped me get into university. I was just another Joe—a commodity. I was healthy now, but if I continued to live on the streets would I be healthy a year from now? America was a Third World country, how long before poverty took its toll on me as it had my parents?

So, what did I care if they married me off? At least it dramatically improved my chances of living to reach Mars and offered me the only chance with a girl I had any likelihood of attaining.

"You'll be bound to ten years' service to Colonial Management and to siring five children."

"Bonus for siring more, they said," I added.

"Yes… There are contingency bonuses that go into effect that cover every conceivable circumstance."

"And the training I'll get is part of the package?"

"Yes, plus food, housing, all covered for your ten years of service… but after that you'll have to earn your own money. Although, what you accrue in bonus monies is yours, free and clear."

"No taxes for the rest of my life?"

"None, or for that of your spouse… Just put your biometric card in the slot and sign here, Mister Grime."

I did. I just hoped I hadn't just chosen to snuff myself.

The next thing I knew sunglasses popped out of a dispenser on my right. "Put on the protective glasses," that dry sounding recorded voice said. "Failure to do so can result in blindness… Proceed along the orange line… Fill the positions one through two hundred fifty on the right and one through two hundred fifty on the left." The doors opened and a line of naked young men entered, allowing me to move forward and take a spot on the right.

I put on the glasses as the recording said, "Doors opening in thirty seconds, twenty seconds, ten seconds. Stand back, doors opening. Enter now."

I swallowed and went inside. The door closed with a thud that sounded as if I was being locked in a tomb. "Stand in the center of the room. Remove your biometric card and place it on the receptacle in front of you. Spread your legs as indicated. Put your arms out to the sides. Under no circumstances remove your glasses. Infrared shower will commence in three, two, one…"

The lights made a crackling sound, or perhaps that

was my skin as the light played around me. When the light went off the chamber reset. "Retrieve your biometric card." The door opened. "Exit now… Proceed along the orange line."

I walked out and dropped the glasses in the waiting receptacle. That's when I realized I was covered in what looked like ash.

"Proceed to the showers," the recorded voice said. "You will have two minutes to shower. Once complete, proceed through the wind tunnel for drying."

Why that sounds like fun, I thought.

There had to be a couple thousand people lined up for the showers. A couple of guys shoved each other. A voice shouted over the intercom, "You are tagged! Any more trouble and you're out!"

No one said a word, and I couldn't really blame them, which only made this all the more surreal.

So like them, I did as I was told and washed the ash off as quickly as I could, luxuriating in being able to wash with real soap, and realized, as I left the showers, that I looked paler than ever. "Put on the medical gown provided. Slip the string over your head. Put on the medical gown provided. Slip…" the recording repeated as I grabbed the backless paper-like gown.

"Proceed along the orange line. Proceed along the orange line."

So, I followed my ten thousand or so new, pinker-skinned friends.

"If you are older than seventeen, continue along the orange lines," the intercom repeated in various languages. "All others follow the blue lines!"

Thus began the med scans, which I prayed wouldn't weed me out. I shook my head, thinking it was funny—after all, I guess all us guys were willing to do just about anything to get lucky.

"Hey! Ouch!" we chorused being give shots for who knew what.

"S***!" I rasped when it was my turn.

15

Chapter 2 – The Deal

I rubbed my backside, and ended up in another long line, which led to a small office where I found myself facing a medico, who asked me about my sex life.

"Practically non-existence," I answered.

The medico didn't even smile at my joke. I guess he heard that a lot.

He swabbed my mouth for DNA and confirmed my understanding that I would be required to give sperm before launch, which would be kept in a radiation proof, nitrogen filled container, along with a sampling of my spouse's ova.

"It would be best if she conceives before the flight, um, Mister Grime… Or if you'd both prefer, she can surrogate for a bonus for each successful birth."

"Uh, can we talk about it first?"

"Your spouse may elect to surrogate before you consummate your marriage. But, then again, you can earn a bonus, too, if you elect to allow us to use your sperm to surrogate another female colonist… You must understand—genetic diversity is critical for human survival in the colonies."

"Uh, yes, Sir… Can I put on some real clothes, now?"

"No." Snap. The medico put on latex gloves.

"Um."

"Please cough for me."

I did.

"Again… Now, please bend over the table…"

"Huh?" Moments later I rasped, "Argh."

I heard another blasted ping, then proceeded down the blue line again, clearly seeing hundreds upon hundreds of people about my age wearing the too short one-size didn't fit all backless paper gowns.

Soon the male and female lines merged, and I heard the first sound from anyone in processing in a long time. A girl giggled, eyes wide catching sight of me. She couldn't have been more than twelve. Well, I guess, like me, a bunch of other the teenage boys tried to nonchalantly cover ourselves based on where we were worst exposed, while the line of teenage girls pacing us on the left did the same.

Their hair was shaved as short as ours. Embarrassed, the girl and I suddenly avoided looking at each other. I didn't know if Colonial Management had a sense of humor or figured they saved money this way.

I shook my head and chuckled with a glance back at the rather scrawny girl. I guess she was right. This was a bit ludicrous. And what was the point? We were getting married soon enough.

In the moment I looked back, she suddenly smiled back at me. I turned away. *Please God, don't marry me to a child!* My life had been miserable enough, thank you very much.

"Proceed and enter the room with your number on the display," the recording repeated over and over.

I stopped before a room on my left, which flashed several numbers including the one on my card.

Hesitant, I entered and found myself alone. Shortly thereafter two other guys entered. Both were a bit older than me, then the door whisked closed and another, across the room, opened. I blinked as two young women came in, stopped and stared at us.

While we stared at each other, the prerecorded voice said, *"Those in this room match your compatibility index. Please use this time to select your spouse. Once you have made your choice, enter your biometric cards in the readers. Your marriage will then be recorded.*

"Food and beverages have been provided for you… Should

you not wish to partner with those offered, remain in this room until a suitable, compatible, partner enters.

"Please be advised that if you do not select a spouse from those offered, Colonial Management may choose one for you who may not be as compatible… However, choice of spouse is your own. Thank you."

We stared at each other, then I said, "Uh, hi, I'm Gary."

"Shelly."

"Tamra"

"I'm Bud."

"Ken."

The girls looked at us as well; we sat down for an awkward lunch, by the end of which I witnessed Bud and Tamra, and Ken and Shelly getting married. I sat there as they left and waited, wondering if I was crazy. After all I was getting married to someone I didn't know in order to survive a process that still had a good likelihood of killing me.

The door opened about an hour later and she walked in.

I stared.

She glared and said, "They've got to be kidding. At least the last three needed a shave."

"The Docs think I'm compatible with you?" my voice squeaked.

"Not a perfect match, but close enough. They showed me your intelligence quotients. You're smart as opposed to the Neanderthals they suggested I shack up with."

"Okay… Um, I'm Gary."

She frowned and nodded, still looking less than pleased.

I couldn't help but think she was beautiful. She was practically an Amazon. But no way was I going to marry, well, a shrew. "Hey, don't do me any favors. I'll wait for the next match.”

She came over to me and raised her hand to my jaw, then checked my teeth. “You actually brush regularly?”

“Uh, yeah.”

She smiled, “The Neanderthals haven’t.”

“So you want to marry me for my teeth?”

She frowned and poked at my skinny right arm “There’s really muscle under there… I’m impressed.”

I thought about prodding her in return, but at her dark look, quickly thought better of that idea. “Okay, you’re looking for someone smart, without bad breath, of course…”

She glared at me.

Nodding, I couldn’t help but ask, “Well, how old are you, anyway?”

“I’m eighteen.”

“You look, uh, older.”

“How old are you?” she asked.

“Fifteen.”

“Jeez. You’ve got to be all hormones.”

I hope so, I thought, fighting that nagging sense that I might have won the genetic lottery.

She shook her head beginning to look really angry, pushed up her bazoombas and said, “So, you think I’m going to be your joy-toy?”

I swallowed, then felt the ludicrousness of the situation, I pointed at the door, “Look, it’s obvious we’re wrong for each other. I’m sure you can find some handsome Neanderthal who favors using a toothbrush before Colonial Management figures you’re out of the program.”

“What?!” she almost shouted.

“Look, this is about marriage and making babies,” I said. “I don’t want to spend the rest of my life fighting with someone obviously as smart as you seem to think you are. Mom and Dad were all for making babies… But it didn't pay the bills. Going to Mars will—and I intend to live through hibernation. So, there's the door, I'll wait for my next less-than-compatible potential mate, thank you very much!"

She walked up to me, put her hands on my face and kissed me. I was out of breath when she said, "Really? Think you can do better than me?"

I felt weak-kneed, but what the hell. I really hate bullies. "You're outta of luck, aren't you?"

She looked shocked, then tears filled her eyes.

Tears? That was a low blow. "Stop that!"

She looked down, "I'm Cindy… But you can call me Sin, everyone else does…" She swallowed hard. "Please, marry me."

"Drop the act!" I hate it when my sisters pulled the tears to get what they wanted.

She wiped her crocodile tears, then stood straighter. "Okay, Gary, bottom line, I'm looking for smart more than horny." Then she looked up. "Lord, does he really have to be fifteen?"

"You're not so special!" I shouted in my own rather lame sounding defense.

Sin hopped up on the table, sat, and crossed her arms. "I've impressive charms."

"Too bad they couldn't do anything about your personality… I take it that's why you ended up here."

She shook her head, "No, I really turned them all down." She gestured at her chest. "They only saw these and never even looked at my eyes."

"Well, they were idiots. You've wonderful eyes." I couldn't believe I actually said that.

She frowned. "You really are looking at me, not just the bod."

"Well, if I'm going to live with you, I want a partner; someone I can discuss things with. Could be worse, you could be illiterate and not even care." I frowned. "You can read, can't you?"

"Yes," she sighed, "I can read."

"Uh, good, I'm not looking for a screaming match every day saying what a waste my wanting to read is. I had enough of that at home." *Well, when I had one,* I admitted to myself.

"Okay, Gary, you're definitely not a Neanderthal. Marry me…"

"Why? Don't tell me you've somehow managed to piss off Colonial Management?"

She looked at me. "No, of course not… I just don't like the idea of having to become a Colony whore. If I am going to have babies for the greater good, I'm going to have them by a man with some brains!"

I frowned, "You're afraid if you miss this trip you'll be too old to survive hibernation to try again."

Shaking her head, Sin hopped off the table and rubbed at a tear in the corner of her eye. "Well, let's say there is some truth to that… and if I just wanted to have kids for the sake of having kids, I could do that here—even with it being against the law to be an unwed mother."

I looked at her. "At least that has some ring of truth to it."

She stared at me.

"Come on, Sin. Having babies is not what this is about. Be honest, what you fear is what that bod of yours will lead you to do—if you're stuck here."

Sin shook her head, and muttered, "Too smart by half."

Chapter 3 – Lucky Me

Okay, Sin, I mean Cindy, was in a bad spot. Too pretty by half and hating the idea of becoming a joy-toy—and not just to a healthy fifteen-year-old who took care of his teeth. She could do a lot worse than me, and knew it.

However, I'm not the most trusting soul, either. I was a survivor and didn't want to get played—or at the very least sell this opportunity short. After all, she was gorgeous.

"You're not like the other guys they tried to pair me with," she said.

"Huh?"

"The last one tried to rape me once we were alone. I decked him but good… I broke his nose."

"He shouldn't have done that…" Not to mention Colonial Management shouldn't have allowed it, I thought. And they seemed like such nurturing types, after all. "You really broke his nose?"

"Yep," she smiled. "Which, truth bc told, hasn't exactly endeared me to Colonial Management, which is why I've this odd feeling that I'm not going to find a better guy than you."

I stared at her, feeling my heart in my throat. "Sin—Cindy… We can die in hibernation."

"Yeah and likely will if it turns out you aren't hetro, Boyo." Then she glanced down and agreed, "Okay, you appear to be hetro."

I grinned, paper clothes didn't hide much, and held up my biometric card with a gesture toward the reader.

She frowned, "Fifteen? Heaven help me." She shook her head, not looking entirely convinced.

I spent some time proving that I was up to the challenge. We lay together on the padded floor. She stared at me, breathing heavily.

"So?" I asked, not certain if it was sweat or tears on my face.

"Um," she said, "I think you've more to prove."

"Huh? Oh!"

We were about to put our biometric cards in the reader when I paused, "Uh, are you planning to surrogate?"

"No, I'll go with your efforts in that regard."

"Huh?"

"You are planning to donate, I hope."

"Uh, no."

"You should."

"Why?"

"The bonus, idiot… You want to be an indentured servant for the next twenty years?"

"What are you talking about?"

"You're kidding, right? Didn't you read the contract's fine print? There are penalties for guys not donating to the sperm bank… They want to assure genetic diversity and should the radiation shielding fail during the crossing that could sterilize a lot of us, so if you're healthy and don't bank sperm for the use of the colony—they doc you ten years."

"And that's not true for girls surrogating?"

"No, that would be immoral."

"Oh," I muttered, then said, "So, I'm just supposed to donate?"

"Uh, not quite… Once we're married I, uh, can help you donate." I smiled. She sighed, "And, there's a bonus for both quality and, uh, quantity."

I looked at her.

She frowned and asked, "You going to marry me or not?"

We put our cards in the reader and got married. I had a partner. I smiled and stared at her great bazoombas.

Sin muttered, "Don't make me regret this, Kid."

The honeymoon lasted over a month at the heavily guarded Roach Hotel in the walled downtown Death Valley. We had a very small room with little more than a good view of the ships being prepped to embark for docking in orbit with the ship that would take us to Mars, a journey that would take about eight months. I figured this was Colonial Management's idea of getting us used to living in cramped quarters.

For the hundred thousand Americans traveling steerage to the New World time was going to pass through the long sleep.

I'll say this for Colonial Management, I'd never eaten so well, or so much, in my life. Yeah, they were fattening us up for the trip, but I didn't care. Sin kept ordering me to slow down, "It's not going anywhere, Kid."

I didn't want to tell her it always had in my corner of the universe. Beautiful young women, like her, likely ate a bit more regularly than I ever had.

The medicos injected Sin with a drug that spurred her fertility before we checked into the hotel.

They harvested some of her ova and took my sperm donation, then told us to enjoy our honeymoon, and that they had left enough ova *in utero* for us to have excellent odds of conception.

Right before launch Colonial Management credited our latest bonuses. The medicos banking my last sperm donation looked at Sin and I oddly, double checking the chart. I only said, "It pays to read the fine print."

"That is does, young man," the last doctor we met with said before announcing, "Miz Grime, you're pregnant with twins. We're crediting you a double bonus."

Sin and I were stunned.

"I must warn you; however, the likelihood is that

only one will survive to be born. However, hibernation at such an early stage of conception has the highest survival odds for newborns."

Soon enough, Sin and I joined the line of those boarding the ships that could be, at best, described as towers with rocket engines strapped on. I couldn't help but think we were about to join the sardines in the big tin can in the sky.

Small duffel bags slung over our shoulders, we went through a final security screening before being led to the main hold where the hibernation chambers were mounted like a bank of rides at an amusement park.

It was eerie seeing them, knowing we were going to be transported in them for months and wouldn't be awake for the launch or transfer to the colony ship in orbit. The chambers were self-sufficient, redesigned from their previous purpose as life support for the otherwise clinically dead.

"Remove your clothing and place it in the receptacle provided," announced a mechanical voice over the intercom. *"All luggage must be neatly stowed. Once sealed inside your chamber will cycle up a level, allowing the next couple to enter this area and board their chamber."*

We stowed our bags, removed our clothes and climbed inside the chamber which had transparent walls and ceiling. We could see other young couples settling in as our hatch sealed and we went on internal atmosphere.

"Welcome, colonists, you are beginning the first leg of your journey across the Solar System. Please be aware that there will be periods of zero gravity;
however, the pod is designed to spin simulating gravity to maintain as much muscle mass and bone density as possible, aiding the bots who will monitor and see to your physical needs during the journey.

"Once you reach Mars Station, you will be subject to

another health exam. Those deemed likely to survive descent onto Mars will be dropped into the new North American Zone as soon as possible, becoming part of the colonial building and terraforming project underway across the planet.

"Please use the port-a-potty at this time and feel free to activate the chamber's rain or fog features to freshen up or enjoy further privacy during the remaining minutes of your honeymoon before hibernation. Also, please do not be alarmed by the bots, which will see to providing you care and sustenance during the journey, particularly the port-a-potty bots, who are your best friends in hibernation.

"Please be advised that it is vital for your safety that you— keep each other warm—as the hibernation process begins… Please look at the hologram for physical positions for—keeping warm—that seem to maximize survival during the hibernation process."

"We are currently boarding twenty-one thousand more colonists. Based on the current rate of boarding, projected time to hibernation activation is… four hours and six minutes... This ship is second
in queue to launch."

Sin and I looked at each other as our cylindrical chamber moved up in sequence. You could not stand up comfortably, but then again, hibernation was intended for sleeping together. We could see a great deal of activity going on in the other chambers and saw young people looking at us, too.

One young man's eyes widened and he glared at Cindy, who turned to me with a hearty laugh and gave me one hell of a kiss. I was left gasping for breath until the chambers cycled away from each other. I suddenly realized the twelve-year-old girl who had been giggling in line was paired with Sin's old friend Chip.

"Don't get me wrong, Sin, but why did you feel the need to put on the show for him?"

"I wasn't. I just realized how lucky I am to have you. Seeing him, well, made me realize that."

I smiled, "In that case." I reached out, offering a hug.

She sighed and drew me close.

"I feel bad for the girl that got stuck with him," Sin muttered some time later as we nestled together.

"Hmm?"

"Chip—the one I, uh, punched in the nose… I hope he learned his lesson and treats that girl he married with respect."

I looked at her. There were tears in her eyes, "Sin, are you all right?"

She wiped the tears away, "Yeah, I'm fine."

"He scared you badly, didn't he?"

"Yeah, I suppose so. I guess if I wasn't getting off Earth, I could expect that kind of treatment every day—and likely would be doing more than breaking the bastard's nose to get rid of him, and his kind."

I looked into her eyes. "Are you really eighteen?"

She shook her head, "No. I lied."

"Uh, good," I muttered.

"I'm twelve and a half." There was an impish sparkle in her eye.

I stared at my wife, "You're kidding."

"Yeah, of course, I am… You think a twelve-year-old could figure out how to game this system and get off Earth without, well, never mind."

"Uh, Sin…"

She had that look that I'd thought of as an angry glare. "What?"

"You're pretty smart, however old you are."

"Yeah, but what good was it going to do me?"

Then, she kissed me again and I saw stars.

"Boarding has now been completed," Colonial Management announced over the intercom. *"The hibernation process will begin momentarily. Please assume your*

positions… Gases will begin sequencing. Do not be alarmed by the odor. Launch will commence in fifteen minutes."

Sin and I had done plenty of, uh, talking and agreed on which position we wanted to hibernate in, having tried all the positions offered in the diagrams at least five times. Okay, twice.

As the gas hissed, we kissed in a lover's embrace. I prayed our twins survived the journey. The idea of being a father was a strange one. New world, fatherhood, not knowing if we would survive the voyage, so many unknowns, but with this woman by my side I thought we stood a good chance of making a better life together on Mars. "I'm lucky to have you, too," I said, feeling so tired and whispered, "I love you."

"Idiot, of course you do," Sin whispered, holding me tighter, kissing me as the gases began to carry us away. As I drifted off I thought I heard her say just before losing consciousness, "I'm so sorry…"

Chapter 4 – Wake-up Call

Hisssss. Bing. I blinked feeling pinches of pain in my arms as the bots retracted into their alcoves, IV lines being sucked in behind them. *"Hibernation cycle complete. Imperative that you rouse your spouse, help warm them... emergency resuscitator set in the floor... Please check on your spouse now in case they died during transit... It is imperative for your survival that you wake up... Strokes and heart attacks have been known to occur during awakening procedure, use the red emergency button to alert Med Control."*

I groaned, my body stiff and lethargic. My mouth feeling gummy. My eyelids felt glued to my face, and my tongue a bit like sandpaper. I took a deep breath and realized the air smelled foul, oh, that was likely just me and, "Sin?"

"Hibernation cycle complete. Imperative that you rouse your spouse, help warm them... If your spouse fails to rouse, use the emergency resuscitator set in the floor... If your spouse died during transit, please press the black emergency button. It is imperative for your survival that you wake up at this time. Increased blood and oxygen flow are essential. Strokes and heart attacks have been known to occur during awakening procedure, use the red emergency button to alert Med Control."

"Hmmm," a cold hand slapped my face.

"Ouch... Sin – dy?"

"Gar – ry?"

Fingers pulled at the fuzz on my face and drew my face close to hers. I blinked, finding it difficult to see clearly. We gave each other a quick kiss, feeling the deceleration giving us a sense of gravity, happy to be alive, laying side by side. "Uck... worst morning... breath... ever," she muttered.

I moved my hands and found, well, a large bulge where there hadn't been one between us. "Sin?" I muttered, struggling to see.

"The twins… Lord, I'm huge, Gary," she replied, lying back.

I nodded, "And I've finally got hair on my chin – and," my eyes opened as I looked at us, "I'm scrawnier than ever."

She chuckled. "The twins trump your not being fifteen anymore."

"Can't say the bots did much for your hair," I offered, reaching back, feeling the stubble atop my head, which matched what the bots had done to hers.

"And I thought they were supposed to be our friends," she sighed.

"Better than finding the stuff having strangled one of us during hibernation, I suppose."

"If you have an emergency, please press the emergency button on either wall. To note your conscious status, please place your biometric card in the slot. At this time you will likely not feel hungry; however, it is imperative that you soon begin drinking water and consume the nutrition paste."

"Doesn't sound appetizing, but I am starving," I said.

"Now that's something we can definitely agree on. Where's the dispenser?" Sin asked. "I definitely need to drink something."

"Colonists typically lose between twenty-five to thirty-five pounds on the trip to Mars. Of course, due to differences in metabolism, you may have lost significantly more, making it imperative to begin drinking water in moderation."

Sin and I soon keyed our biometric cards. Green light suffused the floor as we, uh, warmed ourselves. From our perspective it had been only days since we'd been introduced, before joining thousands of young couples entering hibernation aboard one of the Colonial Management starships boosting into orbit. I've no memory of the docking of the main ship or any of the passage.

So, here I was, a sixteen-year-old married to a

nineteen-year-old, perhaps she was twenty by now, arriving at Mars Station. Then again, "Nine months gone in our slowed metabolic state."

She sighed, "We're definitely awake—you never shut up, otherwise."

I looked at the recorder. "Err, I suppose not." I smiled, retrieving some squirt bulbs filled with water, offering one to Sin.

She took it.

"You're welcome."

She glared at me and patted her stomach, "No, you're welcome."

I drank down the rest of my water bulb to that, then keyed the nutripaste dispenser. "Here."

"Oh, thank you," she said sarcastically; then we ate the bland stuff.

We set the empty water bulbs, the squeezed nutripastes in the recycling unit, then looked at each other. We both could not help but shiver. "Oh, get over here," she muttered, and we cuddled, sharing body heat.

"We really made it." Shaking her head, "And I'm a goddamn balloon!"

We dimmed the chamber lights. The transparent walls and ceiling we fogged. My hair and nails had grown long as had Sin's. The sickly sweet smell of the hibernation gasses still wafted on the air. We both rubbed our arms where the IVs had fed and helped keep us hydrated.

A light flashed minutes or hours later. *"Colonial Management welcomes you to Mars Station. Now that we are part of the station's rotation, please bathe, using available facilities. The timer will now indicate when you will be disembarking; however, please be advised, first priority will be given to chambers in your quadrant with an emergency. Your time will change based on emergency priority."*

"Well, take out the sponges and do my back," she turned about.

"Um."

"Gary, damp sponge first. Soap to follow. Then pass the sponge to me. You know the drill."

I scrubbed her back, sudsing her thereafter and passed her the sponge, getting myself another.

"Turn around, I'll do your back."

The vents sucked the loose water out of the chamber and back into the recycler. We massaged each other's heads and taking the venting nozzle to clear more of the soap and water, which were sucked away.

I turned off the suction, our dampness making us feel all the colder as the fans blew and the ventilation system created wind.

"I hate this," Sin muttered. "I'm so damned cold."

I drew her close, rubbing her back.

She set her head again my shoulder. She blinked. "Did you feel that?"

I grinned, looking down at her belly. "What was that?"

"The babies are kicking."

I grinned, feeling momentarily as if I was in heaven. That, of course, didn't last long. My stomach began to rebel. I grabbed a barf bag.

"Gary!" Sin yelled in disgust.

I rubbed the glass clear after we dressed in what were little better than the paper medical gowns we'd worn when we first met and we peered out at the scores of chambers lighting up green, then started noting chambers lighting up red. Our chamber moved out of pattern as those with an emergency were moved to the head of the queue.

"Gary," Sin whispered.

I swallowed hard, seeing what she did. There were a lot of chambers that simply remained dark. Several began going green, one red, which cycled past us, but far too many stayed dark.

"Ten percent," I muttered.

She winced, "Based on just what I can see, we've easily lost ten thousand people in hibernation," she began to cry, resting her hands around her stomach. "It could have been us."

I thought it still could be. We both looked pretty thin, Sin's bulge or not, Mars could still kill us.

The countdown clock began to feel like a ticking down time bomb.

Our cylinder echoed as the mechanical arm grabbed our unit and pushed us through the lock. Light intensified around us as we entered Mars Station's queue. There was click and a hissing of our atmosphere being released as the plexi-hatch opened.

"EXIT YOUR UNIT, PLEASE."

The low gravity helped. I'm not certain we could have stood, otherwise.

"WELCOME TO MARS STATION. PLEASE FOLLOW THE YELLOW LINE."

Chip looked back, standing there, naked, besides his still too young and now scrawnier looking wife, who glanced back at us over him at me, eyes going wide. "Well, looks like you two are having a successful, uh, marriage," Chip said, less than civilly.

"We're expecting twins," I said.

He blinked.

"You are?" his wife said, unconsciously turning around to stare at me. "Um, uh, congratulations!"

I blinked. "Thanks."

Sin frowned, seeing the bruising on the young woman, still barely more than a girl, and no sign of pregnancy. "Apparently, not as successful a trip for you, Chip."

With a frightened look, his young wife hastily turned around.

The unit hatch closed and they vanished down

what I couldn't help think of as a pneumatic chute. The hatch before us cycled open.

"FOLLOW THE YELLOW LINE."

We were issued sheets, which we shaped in a sort of poncho and marched through the bioscanners. The medico, a woman who had to be in her forties, looked up at us and said, "A healthy set of twins, congratulations!"

To say the least, we were tremendously relieved as Chip and his wife were directed to follow the yellow line.

Sin was put on a gurney. "Mrs. Grime, we're going to have to induce you—encouraging your body to give birth since your metabolism has been affected by hibernating for so long."

"You mean now?" Sin muttered.

The medico nodded. "It's for the best. Gestation is complete. Your children are ready to be born."

"Uh, can I come?"

The medico shook her head, "Mr. Grime, you can be there for the birth, but you've other obligations under your contract at the moment."

"What?" I muttered.

She handed me a cup. "We need to see that you're still viable, young man. Follow the green line, please."

I stared at her as she pushed a button that activated the gurney's motor.

"It'll be all right, Gary," Sin said. "Don't argue, do everything they ask. Lord, you should have read the fine print in your contract."

I sheepishly opened the door of the cubicle they had left me in.

A medico came by, "Finished?"

"Um…" I muttered.

"I'll be back."

"Uh, thanks," I muttered, closing the door. "I think."

I left the medico with the specimen cup. *Sheesh*, I thought, *what had I gotten myself into?* All I'd wanted was to go to the New World and get out of the dregs of a dead end life in the Old Country, the United States.

"Mr. Grime, we need to get you in scrubs. Your wife's water broke and the contractions have begun in earnest."

"Uh, thanks, Doc."

"I'm not a Doc, Mr. Grime. Just a midwife, you have to excuse me, we're in the midst of a literal baby boom—and stay out of the way of the bots, which are monitoring her vital signs."

The medico left me at the entrance to a curtained off room, where I found Cindy glaring at me. "They won't give me drugs!"

"Huh?"

"They said I don't need them," Cindy complained. "We're to watch the bloody vid and I've got you to coach me!"

"Me?"

"Shut up over there. We're tryin' to watch de bloody vid!" a young woman shouted.

I glanced back out the curtain. A guy about my age with a scraggly beard looked back at me and shrugged. "Wonderful," I muttered.

"Gary, this wasn't in the damned contract."

I didn't respond to that. I just turned on the vid, trying not to think about glimpsing Chip trying to make a baby. I don't know which vid was worse. Cindy told me later I fainted in less than a minute.

"Big help you are," a young woman practically yelled only to be echoed a dozen times as midwives rushed between birthing women.

"Mister, uh, Grime," the medico said, glancing at the chart, "do just what they showed you on the vid."

"Me?"

"Help your wife breathe like they showed you. We don't want to perform a Caesarian unless it is absolutely necessary."

"Damn it, give me something," Cindy said, gritting her teeth. "He's useless."

"Ma'am, we've hundreds of babies being born right now and need all the help we can get! Also, we've a limited supply of anesthetic. We use it only when it's warranted."

"This calls for drugs," Cindy rasped.

The medico shook his head, "No, Ma'am. Birth is a natural process."

"Gary, this is all your fault!"

"Uh, yes, dear," it sounded stupid to me, too. "Can I help?"

We turned and stared as an emaciated thirteen-year-old girl in a plastic poncho joined us. "You?" I almost asked her if she was all right.

"They asked if I'd help someone, and, well, you look like you could use it."

The medico nodded, "Excellent way to earn the bonus you need. Put your hand on the biometric reader and help Papa, here, and our new Mama. Press that button when you…"

"I understand." The medico moved to check on someone else. "I, uh, didn't need to watch the vid," the girl said. "I helped my Mom give birth in the Shelter a couple of times. I'm Lisa, by the way," she said to Sin.

"Where's Chip?" Sin said, frowning, realizing who the girl was.

I blinked as the girl frowned. "They're examining him. Then they want him to try earning some bonuses."

Sin nodded, looking at the girl's bruises, which looked worse now than they had, which I was doing my best to ignore as Lisa moved in front of me. "I'm the one who punched him in the, uh, nose," Sin said.

"I know," Lisa smiled. "Now it's time to focus on you." She asked me, "Did you pay attention to the vid?"

"Gary fainted," Cindy replied, disgusted.

"Of course, he did. Well, watch it again, Gary," Lisa said without a hint of ridicule, turning to face me.

"Um, all right," I muttered, turning away to bring back up the vid on the monitor.

Lisa clasped my hand and looked at me, "It's going to be fine. See, she's having a contraction."

Sin gasped, "Argh… That's what this is, Gary, watch that vid! Look at the vid—not me!"

The birth of the twins is something I'll never forget—particularly because Sin won't let me.

Thank Heavens Lisa was there. The place was a madhouse. The medico only came afterward—after Lisa delivered the babies. I'll skip over the fact of how Sin practically broke my hand or how I nearly fainted again. Well, twice.

"Don't you dare drop your daughter!" Lisa shouted, shoving my firstborn into my arms.

When the exhausted looking medico finally reappeared, the babies were laying on Sin's chest. I saw her put ID bands on my daughter and son and claimed there would be measurements to take shortly as several portable med units worked their way around the birthing area with a stack of infant diapers and blankets.

The babies soon began to suckle, though according to the vid, there was little likelihood that any of the new mothers would so quickly be producing milk.

I don't think I can ever explain the look on Sin's exhausted face, the twins lying in her arms. The closest description was a mix of incredulity and, uh, disgust, which I've no doubt was exclusively aimed at me.

Lisa hit me on the shoulder and chuckled, "Congrats, Dad."

"Uh, thanks, I think." I swear, if Sin hadn't been exhausted she would have slugged me.

Chapter 5 – Watch Out for that First Step to Mars

"I hate lines, especially this one," Sin said, as we half floated toward our embarkation point, paralleling nine similar ones all coming down the round hub from the ring of habitats. The conveyor, carrying the transparent balls containing our sleeping twin babies, was suspended on a track over our heads. The flashing orange arrow symbols on the walls, which I suppose should be called the floor, directed us in this section of the station. There was only one couple now ahead of us, and, of course, it was Chip and Lisa, as we approached the egress to our waiting transport tubes that had brought us to Mars.

"Sorry, Sin, I honestly didn't see in the brochure anything about after bringing our huddled asses here, we'd literally be kicked off the space station for our landing."

Lisa and Chip glanced back at us as we paused to retrieve our children from the end of the track before the entrance to their tube rotated into place and the hatch opened, beckoning them. I couldn't help think that Lisa was a good kid, who deserved better than being married to Chip, she had essentially been forced to marry, or lose her opportunity to go to Mars.

I don't think anyone could fault her for not conceiving on the journey, likely too young to, since Colonial Management Medical made certain we were all healthy specimens. I frowned, noticing her bruises still looked far too fresh.

Glowering, said husband, jerked his naked, too young, bride's arm. She cried out in surprise as she found herself propelled in the zero gravity through the open hatch to what had, until recently, simply been referred to as a hibernation tube. A display suspended from the ceiling, counted down how much time remained for them to board before our support tube rotated into place.

The fully automated Mars International Transport Hub, generally referred to as MITH, was working around the clock to drop our ninety thousand properly married teenaged colonists, and surviving young widows and widowers, now being offered the opportunity to remarry to our final destination. I believe we were publicly referred to in the Nets back home as "the scum of the Earth" colonists. MITH felt rather crowded at the moments, crying babies notwithstanding. Bots scurried across the station through maintenance tunnels in the walls which echoed with their passage as they sought to meet our every need, and lately seemed intent on hastening us from our less than spacious accommodations, back to our pods.

The spaceship that had brought us from Earth was now being disassembled and integrated into the station, which one day was planned to be a fully manned orbital habitat, likely offering better accommodations to the Colonial Management staff. MITH would be a main transit point for ships to the asteroid belt, Earth, Jupiter, Saturn, and beyond, or so the newsfeeds claimed.

The station had started out as an unmanned spaceship, which unfolded to become the core of the structure that served as our way point. Our ship's cargo sections had already transited across the outer length of the station's hub down the tracks the life pods now traveled. The cargo sections had already dropped, with one addition to their load: water. An ice covered asteroid had been brought from the belt and was being mined; the ice melted and pumped into the cargo pods, much needed water which we would recycle as best we could to support our growing colony. Now, it was our turn, with our close to thirty thousand newborns.

We entered our all too familiar pod. I passed the

babies in their protective carriers to Sin once she settled inside. I then climbed in and the hatch sealed behind me. The bots inside retracted into the walls. "We're back," I said.

"And more crowded than ever," Sin sighed.

"YOU ARE NOW PART OF THE FIRST WAVE OF COLONISTS FOR YOUR NEWLY ESTABLISHED COLONY," the recorded voice announced. "THOUGH THE UNITED STATES IS THE LAST NATION TO ESTABLISH A COLONY, THAT DOES NOT MEAN YOU ARE BEING PROVIDED ANYTHING LESS THAN WHAT YOUR NATION HAS LEASED TO YOU. YOUR NATION WISHES YOU TO KNOW THAT YOUR LEASING RATE OF THIRTY-FIVE PERCENT IS ONE OF THE MOST REASONABLE AVAILABLE AMONG THE COLONIES. WHEN THE LEASE CONCLUDES IN TWO HUNDRED YEARS, YOUR COLONY WILL BE DEBT FREE AND ABLE TO HAVE A REPRESENTATIVE IN CONGRESS."

"I'm beginning to hate the fine print," I muttered.

Our tube began reorienting, then joined others in what was essentially our ball-shaped survival pod. That's when I saw the spray of water against the transparent hatch. "What the—"

"Waste not, want not," Sin sighed.

"The water was going down in the cargo pods!"

"Well, apparently, we're a cargo pod."

The timer began counting down again.

We checked the babies' safety-netting. Settling into our padding, which had reformed to serve as seats, we strapped in. "At least we can wear the ponchos this time," she muttered. "Though, half floating is worse than awkward."

"I don't know. I kind of like that. You've a nice—"

She glared, "Right, I know you like the view. But you also didn't have to wake up pregnant when we arrived."

"TAKE HOLD. ROTATING IN TEN, NINE…" that hated computer voice went on so cheerfully.

The pod shook as it changed position. Moments later we were stable again. "That was fun," Sin said. "Can't wait for the next part."

Hunched over, looking at the main monitor, the clock counting down on the lower right, I watched the view of some of the asteroids that had been moved into orbit, forming additional moons. "Isn't world cooperation wonderful?" I said, knowing we would pay the price for sending the Earth's poor to terraform Mars or die trying—for our country's getting a piece of the action. What were we hoping to get? Hope itself, I think, having no other.

"Look on the bright side," the recording from Colonial Management had explained, *"most of you are going to make it. The gravity is only about thirty-eight percent of Earth's and you are being dropped into a safety zone built by immigrants just like you, who had a much higher mortality rate before this technique was perfected."*

I looked at our sedated little boy and girl in their gyroscoped safety pods. "Kids, I promise life as a Martian is gonna be better than anything on Earth. We just have to watch out for that first step. It's apparently a doozy."

"Gary, please."

"Yes, Sin?"

"If you want to make it to seventeen, shut up."

"Gary, stop grinning like you think this is funny," she glared.

Our pod shook as it cycled the fifth of the sixth pods our ball could hold, water sloshing against the hatch window. "Come on, Sin, we're in a giant golf ball."

"This isn't an amusement park ride."

"Hey, admit it, Sin. This should be pretty fun until the landing."

"When we, what, go 'smack'?"

"No, you really should have read the fine print about this last leg of our journey. We won't go smack. We are going to begin bouncing across the surface— and into the other golf balls dropping this round."

"ATTENTION: YOUR SUPPORT TUBE HAS BEEN EQUIPPED WITH THE LATEST SAFETY FEATURES IN PREPARATION FOR LANDING ON MARS… BARF BAGS ARE LOCATED FOR YOUR CONVENIENCE IN THE SLOT BESIDE YOU. REMEMBER THE PORTA-POTTY BOT IS YOUR FRIEND."

"Hey!" Sin growled, looking behind her, a tube she knew all too well now snaked— "It pinched me again!"

I grimaced as mine latched into place, too. "Argh, well, remember, the bots are supposed to be our friends."

"PRESSURIZATION COMPLETE. IF YOU SEE A LEAK, IMMEDIATELY COVER IT WITH THE PLATES PROVIDED." I wondered how fun it would be to unharness and try doing that on the way down. Well, at least we'd get the closest thing to a real shower. "TEMPERATURE IN THE UNIT MAY RISE BY SEVERAL DEGREES AND THE WATER OUTSIDE TO REACH THE BOILING POINT. TO AID IN COOLING WE SUGGEST POURING THE RECYCLED WATER OVER YOURSELVES RATHER THAN USE IT FOR DRINKING PURPOSES."

"Gary."

"What, Sin?"

"You've been a better husband than I, uh,

expected.”

"I haven't really done, uh, much." *That was better than admitting I was her last choice for fathering our children.*

She frowned. "I could have done a lot worse…"

That, I didn't doubt for an instant.

"That database you brought for the voyage. It's not filled with the kind of useless facts I figured a fifteen-year-old like you would want."

"I'm not an idiot. Colonial Management likely expected I was bringing computer games and old movies, but the sciences database, alone, should be of enormous help."

She blinked, frowned, "You're pretty smart, but you can be such a jerk."

"Why, thanks, Sweetheart."

Sin looked over at our sedated son's sleeping face. "Think we'll make it?"

"We've made it this far. We'll make it the rest of the way." After that, well, that didn't bear thinking about.

"FIVE MINUTE WARNING UNTIL THE BALL DROPS. ON BEHALF OF COLONIAL MANAGEMENT, WELCOME TO MARS."

I looked down at my daughter's face in the protective ball set near me, "We'll make it for them, and the other children we'll have."

"As if we have a choice about having more children."

"You have to love our Colonial Contract," I replied. "We'll be adding to the gene pool and working for Colonial Management for the next ten years."

"You know they've rigged the deck. We'll be working off our contract for a lot longer than that."

"Of course, I do, Sin. You should look at the colonial histories I've on my database."

Sighing, she said, "Gary, no one's going to mess with us."

"Believe me, I agree wholeheartedly," I replied. "Your prospects back on Earth were as bad, if not worse, than mine. At least this way we've a chance at a better life."

"THREE MINUTES UNTIL THE BALL DROPS. REMAIN STRAPPED IN AT ALL TIMES. EMERGENCY RATIONS ARE LOCATED IN THE BINS WITH YOUR BELONGINGS."

Sin looked at me as we felt the tube shake and begin to rotate with the others, creating a new sense of "down." Water splashing against the unit's transparent hatch window we could see the other young parents in the tube on our left, looking as nervous as we were. I hadn't wanted to glance to the right, but knew I had to look. The broad-shouldered young man next door was glaring at me.

I smiled back, "Chip looks happy to see us."

"His nose still has that broken look," Sin replied, a twinkle in her eyes.

Her prospective first husband looked back at us. "You must have a great right hook."

"Oh, that's just a by-product of him crashing to the floor after what I likely did break," she replied with a vindictive looking crooked smile.

Their unsuccessful first meeting had not endeared either of them to Colonial Management; however, that worked out just fine as far as I was concerned.

I just felt bad for Lisa. She looked back at me wide-eyed as the rotation speed increased, making me feel like we were on some type of old-style roller coaster spinning us around on the track. Lisa looked more like a little kid in that moment, not at all like the confident midwife she had been, not so long ago.

Lisa met my gaze and struggled to give me a smile, looking a bit calmer. She was definitely a survivor, I'll give her that.

I smiled back at her, which made Chip's scowl all

the darker. As our rotation speed increased, we had literally more pressing matters to distract our silent interchange. We were pressed even deeper into our padded couches.

"TWENTY SECONDS UNTIL DROP. ON BEHALF OF ALL OF US HERE AT COLONIAL MANAGEMENT, HAVE A PLEASANT LANDING."

The support tube quaked as we were expelled, spinning in our life pod from the Station. The Station view showed us among ten tumbling life pods being spat away.

The image changed to one of MITH itself; what I suppose might be considered a stylus spinning with four Conestoga wagon-like spoked wheels visible, only three spokes, though. "That view's from our colony ship."

"Oh, how nice of them to share," Sin muttered.

A moment later the signal ended and display deactivated, switching to the image of the Colonial Management Logo with the words "Welcome to Mars" beneath it.

Soon we were both sweating as the temperature rose, bouncing around, restraints straining. "This is a bit more than a few degrees hotter!" Sin grumbled as we sweated.

I would have replied, but was too busy struggling to reach my barf bag.

"Will… we… never… stop… boun—cing?" Sin cried, looking like she was going to puke. But that may have been due to the red lighting that came on at the moment of our pod's impact with the ground.

Well, the first one.

Even in Mars' significantly lower gravity, the jerking against the straps left me gasping, then there was that sudden drop, followed by a jarring impact. I glanced at the support pods with the twins, who were asleep, looking completely unaffected.

I wished Colonial Management would have invested in something like that for us as we rotated in our tube with brief images of our neighbors in a similar plight.

Rolling, the gyros struggling to stabilize us, we gradually slowed before coming to a rocking stop.

The irritating pre-recorded computer voice said, "WELCOME TO MARS. PLEASE REMAIN SEATED. YOUR POSITION MAY NOT BE STABLE BEFORE ALL PODS HAVE COME TO A STOP. COLONIAL MANAGEMENT PERSONNEL WILL RETRIEVE YOU AS SOON AS POSSIBLE."

Feeling dizzy, I said, "I guess this makes us Martians." I wondered what other surprises were in store for us.

"PLEASE REMAIN SEATED. YOUR POSITION MAY NOT BE STABLE. IN ORDER TO INDICATE THAT YOUR PARTY IS UNINJURED, PLEASE DEACTIVATE THE RED WARNING LIGHT, NOW. COLONIAL MANAGEMENT PERSONNEL WILL RETRIEVE YOUR POD AS SOON AS POSSIBLE."

"The kids?" Sin practically croaked.

"They look fine to me. Thank heavens they're sedated. You all right?" I asked.

Cindy nodded, looking pale, smiled grimly, her breathing, like mine, visibly less labored. She began to smile more naturally. She was so beautiful. I was the luckiest man in the world.

She leaned closer to me, straining against her safety harness, as if to kiss me. I leaned toward her in turn. That's when she barfed.

"WELCOME TO MARS," the computer voice droned on. "PLEASE REMAIN…"

"Argh… Yeah, we heard you the first time," I

muttered, wishing the potty bot really was my friend.

"Gary… I'm sorry."

Earth all over again. Literally.

"WELCOME TO MARS, PLEASE REMAIN…"

Part Two: Life on Mars
Chapter 6 – Settling In

Acclimating to the lower gravity, you would think would be easy after having been on the space station, but the gravity there was stronger than here. We shivered in the dry air as our guide led hundreds of us to our new living quarters in District Thirty-Three. We held poles latched to the side of the protective gyro balls the kids slept in. I also dragged our assigned travel cart behind us with what belongings we had. That meant two small duffel bags.

Taking us across the main corridors of warren, the subtran system was for emergencies only, needing a lot of power to operate and our guide made clear, "The colony needs to conserve every watt. Using more than your allotment will debit your years of Service."

"Oh, joy," Sin whispered.

We passed cross-corridors with signs with arrows that read "Geothermal Power Plant," "Farming 6," "Manufacturing 4." I got a sense of just how large the colony must be, then again, the underground colony was a city on Mars, somewhere on Mars.

"I wish we weren't underground and could actually see the world out there."

Sin chuckled, "You're right, I'd love to see the ocean out there. Oh, right, there are only rocks or we could get a great view of solar panels, no doubt."

The walk was long and gave us the opportunity to learn to walk and stop bumping into each other, and the walls. To be honest, walking was more like shambling to me. Our guides wore pressure suits and showed us how to cycle through each of the hatches between sections, warning, "Never enter a red lit section without being fully suited and without checking your tank. And don't enter such a section without a plan as to how you plan to fix whatever killed everybody."

There was laughter at that remark, not from Sin and me, though, our guide's hair was gray streaked, but her face looked only about ten years older than ours.

Our guide shouted, "You lot, quiet, we've arrived at the lock to District Thirty-Three East. Plenty of time to enjoy dreaming about hours dusting off the solar panel arrays." Keying, the lock, "If you're that lucky one day… Oh, I forget, Thirty-Three is also known as the Grubber District. You'll understand all too soon. And kiss the very idea of seeing the sky again goodbye."

"Grubber?" someone muttered.

I sighed, answering, "We'll be creating new sections of the warrens."

Our guide gestured us to proceed, "Don't dawdle, welcome to Grubber's Alley," voice cold. "You, there, the apartments on the other side are for you lot. Put your hand to the biometric pad to key them. And no reason to get picky, they're all identical."

"And be smart, watch the goddamned vids—and, after this moment, never go anywhere without your pressure suit."

Sin and I glanced at each other, we were in no rush to select any of apartments closest to the hatch as families splintered off. Our guide noticed, did not comment, and led us on through the section, telling us, "Grubbing isn't the worse Service. Be smart, watch the vids and you might be all right."

Corridor Eight was only distinctive because it was marked by an "8," which seemed almost freshly painted, and I thought might actually glow in the dark. The lights were not strong here, but I thought that might be deliberate. The illumination was getting dimmer by the hour as the thousand or so of our neighbors crossed the underground warren, glimpsing only the Meeting Chamber, one of a dozen, we were told.

Sin gestured. We keyed the pad and accepted our apartment. The door whisked shut behind us. The lighting was dim. The switch to change that was not apparent. Oh, well, it was enough to see by, at least.

We took the twins out of their protective cocoon balls. "I hate the idea they've had so many sedatives," Sin said.

"Well, you may appreciate it more once it wears off," I offered.

Sin looked at me, "I know." She held our daughter, and me, our son, looking around. There were our pressure suits behind plastic curtains, with tear-away seams, which seemed to cover all the walls. I moved to the section in the rear and one handed, eased a seam open, "What the—"

A transparent tube was built into the wall and fish swam past. Above it were hydroponics lines with vegetables, not yet ripe, hanging down from them. "Well, we won't starve."

"Not immediately," Sin said. "Or do you know how to keep them growing?"

I went over to the vid, tapped it.

The Colonial Management logo appeared. "WELCOME, MR. AND MRS. GRIME."

A menu appeared on the screen. I touched "Orientation 1."

"WELCOME TO YOUR NEW HOME. YOU LIVE IN WARREN THIRTY-THREE, CORRIDOR EIGHT, APARTMENT SIXTEEN. YOUR APARTMENT OFFERS THE FOLLOWING STANDARD AMENITIES… ONE MINI-KITCHEN WITH ELECTRIC WARMER. WARNING, FIRE IS NOT PERMITTED IN LIVING QUARTERS. ONE MASTER BED, TWO

FOLDING CHAIRS, ONE WITH ROCKING CHAIR MODE. PLEASE SEE INSTRUCTION CARD BENEATH THE SEATS. THERE ARE PULL OUT CRADLES AMONG THE OTHER ITEMS, LIKE SPOONS AND FORKS, AND CLOTH DIAPERS, SONIC CLEANER FOR CLOTHING AND PULL OUT SONIC SHOWER… THE PORTA-POTTY BOT, OF WHICH YOU ARE FAMILIAR, HAS BEEN MODIFIED FOR THE MARTIAN ENVIRONMENT. PLEASE CONSULT THE INSTRUCTION MANUAL BESIDES IT FOR CLEANING INSTRUCTION AND REPAIR… YOUR WASTE IS VITAL TO THE COLONY AND WILL PROVIDE NECESSARY NUTRIENTS FOR THE HYDROPONICS UNIT."

I hit pause. "Well, we have a lot of room back here."

Sin came over and peered past. "Of course, you found the bedroom."

"Well, it's a bed at least. Calling it the bedroom." Moving the curtain aside, I pulled the thin folded mattress off its storage shelf as Sin pulled open the drawer with the pullout bed frame. I unfolded the mattress across it once the frame was fully extended.

"Not much space with this out."

"But we've the privacy curtain."

"How nice of them."

The vid droned on, "THIS CONCLUDES ORIENTATION ONE, COLONIAL MANAGEMENT ENCOURAGES YOU TO TAKE THE SCHEDULED TOURS OF THE COLONY WARRENS AND TO CONTINUE VIEWING THE ORIENTATIONS. TAP TO PROCEED WITH THE NEXT ORIENTATION."

I laid down on the bed to see if it was comfortable and tapped the mattress. "Ready for the next orientation?"

Sin glared at me, "Not now, loverboy. If you've that much energy, start walking on the treadmill and generate electricity for the batteries."

I shook my head, smiled, "Time enough for that later," I sighed. "The bed's not particularly comfortable, anyway."

"No surprise there."

I got up and put the mattress and bed frame away as Sin continued to explore our room, thinking of it as a true apartment, as home, was going to take a while.

Sin turned on the vid, which offered a view of a subterranean farm, and the menu guide below. "I guess this is the best view we are going to get."

I touched the screen and the view changed, offering a red rocky image of the Martian vista. I switched through the interior colony views, a map layout focused on our corridor and section appeared. "Well, this will be helpful, at least."

Sin said across the room behind another plastic curtained section, "This is more helpful," pulling out the retractable shelves that served as cradles for the children. "Oh, nice, some folding chairs. Now, make yourself more helpful and find where the kitchen unit is hidden. There should be a pump for my breast milk around here."

Shaking my head, I replied, "Yes, dear," looking around, searching. When I couldn't find it, I looked back at the vid and scrolled the menu guide and found the schematic for the apartment. "Ah, it's that wall over there."

I pushed the section of wall in, heard a hissing sound, then the wall swung outward. A hot plate was built into the swinging wall, flipping down. The pump and baby bottles were set on the side shelves, plastic sippy cups, well, that's what I thought they looked like were racked next to them, as well as plastic looking plates of a familiar hue. "Well, apparently nothing's going to waste. These are made out of hibernation pods.”

A refrigeration unit was, essentially, the inset wall.

One of the babies began to stir in their sleep.

“Ah, we really should name them, you know,” Sin said.

“What? You don’t like calling them, Thing One and Thing Two?” I sighed, Colonial Management hadn’t encouraged any of us naming our children, yet. That advice was something none of us wanted to think about.

Watch orientation, feed, burb, and evac the babies’ porta diapers. Eat an MRE. We had been allocated ten meals and scores of nutrient bars, plus recycled water, which even Sin agreed tasted a bit salty as if we might be drinking our own sweat.

When the babies settled to sleep in their cradles, their porta diapers latched on to the inset vac in the wall. I turned down the already dim lighting control, the vid identified, to “night light.”

Once I was certain Sin was asleep, I did my best to slip as quietly as I could from the bed.

I knelt and rummaged through my duffel and drew out my trusty Swiss Army knife. Well, it wasn’t actually one, but it might as well have been. It was a folded up multi-tool that was as precious to me as the small computer database with my game looking reader.

I went over to the vid and noted the small camera, which I pried out, then opened up the vid’s panel. I clicked the little LED light on my multi-tool and judged which components were not actually part of the vid. I pulled the components I knew shouldn’t be there and smiled.

“Gary, what the Hell are you doing?”

I chuckled. “Well, I may have learned a thing or two that isn’t in the any database.”

She stared at me.

"Well, I thought you'd appreciate some privacy from now on," I smiled.

"What?"

"The vid's been recording us since we arrived. It hasn't been tapped for viewing yet, at least, I don't think so."

"What? What are you talking about?"

"Sin, uh, I don't want us being spied on, at least, not in our own home."

"Gary, where did that screwdriver thingy come from?"

"This? I hid it in a compartment I rigged in the reader casing."

"And Colonial Management didn't scan that?"

"They check for explosives, drugs, and only care about our weight allowance."

"Gary, how did you even know what to do with the vid?"

I frowned. "Sin, this tech is old stuff. I used to slip into junkyards and rebuild vids just like this."

"Huh? You stole stuff."

"Sin, I was an entrepreneur—the stuff was junk. Nobody cared. So, I, well, made stuff."

"And made enough to buy the database."

"Of course…"

"But how do you know that even had spy features?"

"You're kidding…"

She frowned.

"You do know that recording devices were put in computer monitors and used to unobtrusively spy on users until…"

She nodded, "The Blackmail Scandals."

"This particular old model vid is also easy to print and assemble."

"You know that how?"

"That actually happens to be in my database—and likely reading."

She stared at me, then glanced around. "Gary, you think that's the only recording device?"

"What else would they need? It's simple and cost effective. I take it you've noticed this place isn't exactly new."

Nodding, "This place is supposed to be the first American colony."

I merely met her gaze, knowing she's wasn't fooled.

"The cradle has scratches. It looks well-worn—and the colony… It's huge."

"This whole section of the warrens, alone, is more than made to order — and with the kids there are over a hundred thousand of us. This place took decades to build."

"Gary, I knew you were no fool." She came over to me. "What are you up to?"

"I couldn't exactly consult the database without them knowing."

She stared at me, then kissed me before turning around and going over to the bed.

I stared after her.

"Coming back to bed?"

I blinked and didn't have to be asked twice.

Chapter 7 – On a Good Day You Can See Mars

I went on one of the tours the Elders offered. They worked in teams, clearly not trusting us not to get ourselves killed passing through the pressurized transfer points, sealed against anything going wrong from one section to another.

The farm fields stank to high heaven, obviously benefiting from the fertilizer of the waste treatment plant, but left me wondering how long it had taken to create such a farm, which the government must have considered a major asset in agreeing that this would be our colony.

"Remember, nothing goes to waste," our guide said, gaze lingering on each of us, the far too few tourists.

"The ecology of a colony is intertwined. Each aspect is needed for you and your families to survive. Lose capacity here, and you are all dead. So, treat those assigned here to keep you fed real well. Other colonies didn't, and they died."

Truth, if I ever heard it for someone in their twenties.

I suppose what surprised me most as the tour continued was the sad fact that so few people chose to take the complete tour. The Elders seemed not to be surprised at all. I took the opportunity to get to know the other rather curious among my colonial colleagues.

Those assigned to the various districts were responsible for maintaining different resources or work duties. Most on this tour were young men, with the exception of a number of young women, who, I suspected, like Chip's wife, Lisa, the only other person on this tour from District Thirty-three, who had not been pregnant during the crossing.

I glanced at my neighbor, who was not particularly

talkative on the tour, only saying "hi" to me in response to my saying "hi" to her. But she did seem as curious about the place as I was—and most of my fellow tourists. The exceptions were those who looked bored, who seemed like actual tourists, rather than anyone curious as how to know whatever we could to stay alive and not get anyone else killed.

We proceeded on, but never were taken to restricted areas like the power plants, recycling, or waste management, a place I was actually happy not to visit. "Cycle us through to the next section," the Guide said to me this time.

I did not need to look at the ubiquitous instruction card after being shown, repeatedly, the process. I looked at the card anyway, and noticed something was different. This transfer point was older and worked slightly differently. I followed the instructions, after double checking that the system itself was properly functioning.

"Good, people. Our friend here, had expected this hatch to work like the others we have been through could easily have depressurized the section. This is a much older section of the warrens, leading to what is the core of the colony. This will be a restricted section and only available to those assigned from District One, who will be extensively trained on the systems.

"What they have been told is that should they not meet our expectations they will be reassigned to other Districts that Colonial Management deems more appropriate. So, know that this is true for all of you, here. If we deem you are not meeting our expectations in your assigned areas, you and your families will be moved to another district and to responsibilities, where you will meet Colonial

Management's expectations. Understand me? This colony succeeds or dies based on you meeting those expectations and that means: you and your family live or die."

Wonderful, and likely get others killed in the process. Lovely thought.

Then we got our tour of what I thought of as "Elder" Central, rather than Colony Central before returning to our District, leaving me to ponder, afterward, whether coming to the new world was just a faster way to die, or not.

"Yanks," said the Elder in the white jumpsuit; a woman, who if she were yet thirty, would have surprised me. "Welcome to your community orientation." She stood on the stage at the District amphitheater framed by arching walls crowned by the reinforced domed earthen looking ceiling, "you have had your time to settle in and now playtime is over."

The tiered concrete formed ample seating for the literally tens of thousands of new colonists, none of whom really had a clue about what to do, or expect.

I stood beside Cindy amid my thousand or so neighbors, baby gyros propped open beside us, while the sound of crying babies provided the chief distraction.

"We have shown you the basics of living within these warrens. But there is much more you need to understand, starting with doing what we say—or die. This place is lethal."

Sin and I glanced at each other, holding one of our newborn babies in our arms. I glanced at Chip down a level below us, seated with Lisa, whose arm he gripped, holding her close likely to whisper how disappointed he was at their not having a baby with them.

Lisa winced, glanced over her shoulder. Mouth clamped shut, eyes watering, when she noticed Sin and I watching her. She hastily turned her head and looked down.

"He's hurting her," I whispered, baby cradled,

wishing I could punch that bully of hers in the nose as Sin once had.

"He'll get what he deserves one day," Sin whispered as the baby began to fuss. "Smile, Gary, we don't want to upset the kids."

"I just wish I could do something. It's not right."

Sighing, "No, it isn't. But it's not our problem."

I nodded, dreading having to work in the same division with him, having seen my name and his on the list from what was termed here as "Grubbing."

From the stage the black-haired colonial rep's amplified voice continued her orientation speech. "…In addition to not entering any restricted areas, here are your 'Survival Tips,' which I clearly need to explain to you since so many, apparently, either have skipped watching the vid orientations or were not taking them seriously. So, let me be blunt: Go outside and freeze without a suit. Go outside in a suit for too long and learn to glow. Oh, and do not forget to check your tanks. No oxygen is as bad as is having the wrong mixture." She went on like that for a time, leading to more pragmatic warnings, "Always secure the section hatches. Protect your environment. Let someone else die fighting for air. If you boys like getting into fights, go ahead. Fight among yourselves; kill yourself, and every idiot who happens to be around you."

The woman sighed. "You may be wondering why you have been encouraged to make so many babies… It's because so many of them are going to die and so many of you are going to get yourself killed that this colony just might survive and turn a profit one day. If not, I'll likely give this talk to another group of newbees in a few years.

"Oh, you think I'm trying to be dramatic? My orientation team and I are living in our pressure suits because we trust you'll do your level best to accidentally get us, and all the rest of you killed. That more than half of you are not wearing your pressure suits, prove you are trusting to luck and will likely die because of it."

Sin whispered, "Thanks for reminding me to wear my pressure suit."

"Uh, let's get the kids back into the pods," I whispered.

We did, as the Elder continued, "Yanks, you had best learn to be paranoid enough to survive the stupidity or the failures of systems you are responsible for.

"If you thought getting here had good odds, surprise, the odds are totally against you. For each of you and your entire families who manage to kill yourselves, that will leave more resources for the rest of you… Don't expect any help from your neighboring colonies, who are hundreds if not thousands of kilometers away. They'll only trade with successful colonies like themselves. That improves their odds. And on Mars, we only bet on 'sure things.' And we do what we do to fulfill our contracts to Colonial Management, so we can enjoy the fruits of our labor.

"Which brings me to talk to you about your resources. Your air and water are more precious than anything, I suspect you understand that lesson. Recycling is not a game. Nothing can be allowed to go to waste. If you accidentally destroy something, or don't fix what is broken fast, you are going to die or kill a lot of your fellow colonists, if not your families.

"We have set you up with back-ups for what we could. Do not depend on them. If you do not learn to keep everything going, if you do not pay attention to what we teach you about repairing them. You leave us to clean up before the next colony is allotted what resources are offered.

"Now, time for another aspect of wonder of having babies to provide you incentive not to screw up… Yanks used to have canaries in the coal mines.

Babies are rather sensitive to their environment. As they die, you'll learn the lessons we are trying to teach you—lessons we learned losing our babies, our children. Oh, you thought my friends and I are not sincere in trying to teach you how to survive?

"You think I'm exaggerating? That's what we thought the Elder, who was twenty-five, addressing my colony, was during the orientation address we were given." She shook her head. "We lost ninety percent of our babies within six months. Those responsible did not die quickly enough, I thought—I lost my baby in two months. You newbees, ignore my warning… We're training you as penance for our stupidity."

There was silence — even the babies, in that moment, did not make a peep, which was truly eerie.

"My companions are giving this address in all the other Districts. I hope you are listening. I want to laugh, because I know most of you still are not certain I am not lying. So, do not believe me and likely will laugh after I finish the talk, telling your spouses and buddies I was just trying to scare you… Do not believe it. Listen to the vid orientation in your apartments, over and over—every single educational program Colonial Management offers.

"You can key in myriad documentaries or demos that demonstrate all the ways you can die if you don't check for telltale signs of oxygen loss, atmospheric pressure loss, carbon monoxide poisoning—all of which cannot only bring your lives to a grisly end, but those defenseless little tikes you have given birth to as well."

That brought an awkward silence.

The rep pitched her voice slightly. "We have heard it all. We do not have time to listen to all that claptrap… It is so boring… It can never happen to us." She paused. "There is a family of you Yanks from this

District not here this afternoon. You see, their quarters suffered a failure of the aqua-culture system that both runs through your apartments and provides oxygen through the seaweed that helps feed the fish and filters the, uh, impurities the fish leave behind.

"Apparently, they did not pay attention to the warnings about the transparent tubing. The one to report any sign of cracks." She shook her head. "The crack grew so large that the pressure broke it. As their room was sealed, their entire apartment completely flooded, drowning them. Only reports from neighboring apartments that the water in their tubes was gone alerted Central there was even a problem. That alert came hours too late for the drowned family."

The family's name and apartment location flashed on the screens on either side of the Colonial Management rep. She went on in that way for a good fifteen minutes. Cindy glanced at me, complaining that I was spending too much time watching to the videos and their safety tips.

I didn't think she thought that now. Oh, don't get me wrong. Cindy was smart. She had read the fine print of our colonist contract to a degree I hadn't. That fine print could leave our family in perpetual poverty. After learning of my mistake, I hadn't taken a little thing like ignoring the vid lightly. My favorite part of the lecture, or perhaps this was the pep talk, came at the end when the rep said, "This is not Earth… is not the America you knew. On a good day you can see across Mars, but ignore the weather forecast and literally get blinded and lost by what we call a Salty. That's when the winds blow upwards of 100 meters per second turning the entire planet into a single storm. Oh, the storm itself won't kill you. The gravity's too low and atmosphere too thin. Wandering off blindly will, though. Lost and no oxygen in your tanks makes you the equivalent of a fish out of water back on Earth.

"Think these rules are silly? These are not my rules. These are the lessons learned from the deaths of countless immigrants settling here before you. Obey all the rules or die for your stupidity, it matters not to us in the long run. Colonial Management has more people willing to die for the opportunity to be here—as you all well know."

We looked at each other.

"Now, those assigned as Grubber teams will meet at your designated areas in one hour. Fabricators in ninety minutes, and all other assignments in two hours. I encourage you not to trust your teammates not to get you killed. You've all important work to do—and, believe it or not, we do want you to succeed. It's far less messy… Oh, and this final reminder from Colonial Management, pay attention to your contract and your babies."

Sin glanced at the babies in their pods.

"They are a precious resource, who depend on you—all of you. We need as many of them to survive as possible. The colonization effort will depend on them one day—as it depends on you now. Welcome to life on Mars. Where life itself is a precious commodity."

An Elder was assigned to train my team. He told us to call him Sarge. If that didn't make our relationship clear enough, he certainly sounded like a drill instructor.

He made it clear we were the bottom of the Martian food chain, literally. He told us to put on the vacuum suits we were issued, over our pressure suits. Before I did, I checked the oxygen tank.

Sarge waited a moment, then began shouting at those who had missed that step. "Newbees, always check your tank and the mixture! Don't for a moment think going out there in a pressure suit will keep you alive for more than five minutes!" He peered at my name tag, chuckled, "Grime, you've the perfect name for a Grubber. Now, tell me that when you checked your tank, you actually knew what the levels and mix should be!"

"Yes, I did, Sarge!"

"You, there," he looked at Chip of all people. "You wisely checked as well. Tell your teammates, what those readings should be."

He shouted back, "My air shows full, Sarge!"

"And the mix?"

Chip hesitated.

Sarge glared, "Do your homework! The wrong mix can kill you! Grime, what's the proper mix?"

I shouted back the answer.

Sarge nodded. "You might survive the day, Grime. Now, get those vac suits on, people."

Low gravity did nothing to help my balance one bit after strapping the tank on. I leaned forward to compensate and ended up on my knees, which was better than my teammate on the right, who fell on his face.

"Check your seals, and for cracks in your faceplate," Sarge said rather loudly, which is when I realized I needed to adjust my helmet comm's volume.

Once Sarge inspected us, he told us to prepare to cross into vacuum. He cycled the hatch, which opened into a long corridor, "Come on, people, we do not have all day!"

We followed him into the dimly lit area, bumping into each other. "Come in everyone, so we can begin depressurizing."

I quickly found myself pressed up against a featureless wall and had to remind myself to breathe normally. *I can do this.* Sin and kids need me, which was not what had led me to Mars. That was taking the only chance I thought I had, now, the twins and Sin were wrapped up in it all. It was now all our lives at stake.

Sarge said, "Depressuring."

Soon enough we were entering, well, it wasn't a cavern, exactly. I guess you'd call it the mine. I looked up. The ceiling was about two feet above my head and wasn't cut uniformly.

"People, this area has been carved, out so you have a starting point. The schematic for what needs to be done is available on your helmet display. Just access the suit's menu. Another thing to know, your display will automatically warn you when you have less than twenty percent of air left. However, be smart, check your levels yourself. The displays have been known to glitch and give people no warning at all."

He gestured to the equipment set in a row of open cabinets. "Collect a Grubber's Best Friend, a sonic regulator."

We each took one. Chip almost hit me with the shovel looking end of his, the guy on my right grabbed my arm and pulled me just in time. "Um, sorry," Chip said, though, I could see him smiling through his faceplate when he did.

I glared back as Sarge shouted, "Be careful with those! And don't turn yours on before I tell you to! Now, line up!"

I glanced at the suited guy, who pulled me clear, his name tag read B. Bills. "Thanks, Bills."

"Name's Benny… I've got your back."

"I'm Gary."

He nodded, and we made certain to stand nowhere near Chip.

"The regulator is your shovel. But far more dangerous." Sarge turned and pressed his regulator against the wall in front of us. Suddenly, dirt and rock were torn away. That stopped the moment he backed away. "The sonic regulator will help you carve out new sections, and shape chambers and new apartments based on the schematic. Use the scoop section on the back end of the regulator to place the dirt onto the conveyor, which will put it into the sifting machine, over there. That dirt will feed the fabricators and the teams who are assigned to them. The hatches and materials they fabricate will be used by other work crews to complete the rooms and structures you are hollowing out.

"The shovel end of the regulator, or the sonic side, brushing up a vacuum suit can kill someone, tearing the suit. So, I cannot stress enough the importance of visually checking not just your suit, but the suits of those around you.

"If you feel dizzy, turn off your regulator immediately and check your suits, particular for pressure loss. You have patch seals, basically bandages, in the suit pockets. Check those pockets to make certain you have those emergency patches. The larger sizes are in your leg pockets, smaller are at the arms. They are the same type you have for your pressure suits, which if you are feeling dizzy can indicate your pressure suit has been punctured or torn, as well."

Sarge worked with each of us and explained how to recognize mineral elements amid the dirt and rock, which the filtering system would also shunt aside for the colony's other needs, which the fabricators use to extrude supports, air locks. Another of silica quality would be shunted for making into translucent piping, and more. "Now, we'll break into teams and those in front will use the sonic regulator at the lowest settling, while I work with the rest of you on fabricator and conveyor operations."

I checked my sonic's settings, then glanced over to the kid next to me, who turned his sonic to the highest settling.

"We're supposed to work on the lowest setting only," I said to the kid.

"What's the fun in that?" he chuckled. "I want to

see what this thing can really do."

Idiot, I thought. "Hey, guys," I said, turning to the others on our crew, "our pal here is going to get himself killed. I'm going to work over there, and do it right. Figure, he's going to be dead in a couple of seconds because he knows better than Sarge. I suggest you do the same."

Sarge glanced our way. "What's going on over there?"

It was almost funny first seeing Benny follow me, then the group split up. Over half followed me, well, likely Benny, who was bigger than me. The rest stayed with the brainiac.

"Our friend, there, has put his to maximum."

"Everyone get clear of him fast!" Sarge warned.

The kid laughed, turning to face us, "He showed us this doesn't do nothing unless we press it against it the rock!"

"Don't activate that!"

So, of course, he did.

The base of the sonic dipped to the floor, brushed it, making it burst apart, flinging the kid backward into the wall. His hand holding the regulator trigger was flung to the right, brushing one of those near him, before smacking against the wall, sending dirt and rock spraying everywhere.

Only his hand, being knocked away, turned off the regulator.

Sarge explained emergency procedures as several Elders with Emergency Services and Colonial trainees arrived. They took the kid's body away. The one who had been more than brushed by the regulator didn't live long, thankfully. The suit was pretty much intact, which Sarge explained was more due to the quality of the vac suit.

A half dozen others who had stayed by the kid's

side and not heeded my warning had taken suit damage by the rock spewed at them. But we patched their suits quick enough that Sarge assured us they'd live.

The emergency crew dealt with the mess as Sarge showed us how to "assess the damage" so we could get back to work. "Survival of the fittest, people," Sarge said. "Think you are smarter than me? That is a great way to kill yourself… But understand this, my job is to teach you how not to kill yourselves or those around you. You have a job to do—and the shift is nowhere close to being over, but if you are an idiot, you will be dead rather quickly.

"You lot are alive and unhurt because you either moved away from the fool as soon as Grime, there, correctly warned you—or were lucky enough to be nowhere near him when he decided to commit suicide."

He pointed at the damage done to the kid's regulator, showed us how to check our regulators for damage due to the spewn rock. "There are times when you will need to use the regulator at maximum… I will demonstrate when and how you safely do that when the time is right. Now, anyone else, who wants to play cowboy with the equipment?"

There were no takers.

Sarge said, "Grime, as you and your friends are not dead yet, go shovel onto the conveyors all the debris. We will get back to using the regulators against the wall after everything has been cleared. Oh, and, everyone, stay clear of that gouge in the floor. We will be learning how to compact and repair warren floors a bit sooner than planned, but not this shift…"

"Who is going to tell the kid's wife?" someone asked at the end of the shift while we were waiting for pressurization.

Hearing that Sarge said, "That's already been

handled. His wife will be offered a new marriage before you get back."

I blinked.

"Can… can we visit the injured in the hospital?" someone asked.

Sarge paused before answering, "Hospital? You must have misunderstood, and not checked the colony's schematic. There's a maternity ward here, but no hospital. You get hurt, you heal at home—or best—hope you die quick. Your family will not appreciate accruing years of Service due to your lack of productivity."

No one spoke after that. I knew my fellow grubbers would be paying better attention to the orientation vids tonight. And, if they did not realize it already, gain a better understanding about what it meant that nothing goes to waste.

The dead were recycled like everything else.

Sin heard me come in, looking up from breastfeeding. "How was—" she stopped.

"Tough day." I went to the vid and brought up the data, because that's how Colonial Management treated such news. It listed how many died today from each district. Just under one hundred people. *Huh*.

"His name was Calvin."

Chapter 8 – Safety Tip: It Pays to Be Paranoid

Training took a month. Idiocy was now not completely due to foolishness. Two died from mixture issues their suits didn't report.

"Grime," I heard as I went with my suited crew through the lock into the new section we were building the next day. Most of my crew continued down the main corridor we had been as Sarge called it, "shaping." A figure, regulator in hand, hung back from where his shiftmates had been working a side corridor.

I hated that particular voice. I looked up at him. "Hi, Chip…"

"Heard you ended up the boss of your shift."

"Heard you're boss of your shift, too," I replied.

"Yep… scheduled for the shift after yours. So, don't screw up. I don't want to lose any of mine due to yours screwing up by the numbers."

"Don't worry about my people holding up our end… Just remember that the fabricator is set to fab walls and supports—not build you a giant indoor beach and swimming pool so you can get girls."

"Cute, Kid… How's the wife?"

"Cindy? She's fine… So are the twins. How you doing on your quota?"

Chip shoved me, glaring, "You're really not very bright. Watch your back."

"You do the same."

Shaking his head, Chip chuckled, "I'll see they put that on your tombstone."

One of my boys came back, "I heard that. You know none of us gets a tombstone."

"As they say, 'nothing goes to waste,'" someone muttered.

"We'll be lucky to be notated on the colonial database…"

"Bet you thought being promoted to Boss an honor."

"I'm honored you came back to check on me," I replied.

"Like Sarge always says, check the suits of those around you," Benny said. "Just like you've been doing, mine and other guys, well, we went to Sarge and recommended you, Boss."

I stared at him in surprise.

"We just wanted the smartest guy in charge," one said.

"Just don't be getting a swelled head, though, Boss," another smiled.

Sarge went over the settings on the main fabricator, made us strip down and double check our grubbers' "little friends" then said, "Set those aside for repair and, you boys, take those spares… Remember, I'm not always going to be here to wipe your noses. I've a colony of my own to get back to, and this training is costing your people a lot of credits… Now, check the schematic for this shift and meet your schedule. One day, your people are going to need this part of the warren."

Shift after shift we carved out and fabbed section after section. On my way back home, cycling back into Thirty-three, well, I guess it was officially night, a slight figure blocked my way. I took a step back only to realize it was Chip's wife. "Lisa?"

"Gary, you've pissed him off, bad."

"Huh?"

"Your shift is on CM's list as up for promotion."

"What are you talking about?"

"Someone overheard Sarge praising your leadership and the work of your group. The advisors plan to promote the best… you're the best."

I frowned. "Lisa, why are you telling me this?"

Shaking her head, "You don't get how much Chip hates you. As it takes it out on me for no reason… seems only fair, I for once deserve the treatment."

I blinked. "Lisa, okay, come on. Why are you taking a stupid chance to tell me this?"

She shrugged. "You're nice. You don't deserve it— and, well," she shook her head, "you're kinda cute."

"Huh."

"Look, I gotta get back. Chip's up to something. If I were you I wouldn't trust anything on your next shift." Then she ran off, leaving me staring, not knowing what to think, but suspecting there was no harm in being more paranoid than I already was on a planet where the smallest mistake could kill you.

The guys grumbled at the beginning of next shift at my order to double check everything. Well, the grumbling stopped when we found damage to three of the Grubbers Best Friends. "Gary," Benny said, "the settings have been switched to make the low setting maximum."

"Get the spares and note those three must be repaired, then after the inspections are finished let's get back to work."

"Sure, Boss…"

The next shift we had no spare regulators or replacement parts for those regulators we found subtly damaged. "We're going to work with less regulators, people, and share them. I want us pulling replacements off-duty and repairing them ourselves. Oh, take the ones that failed inspection home, if need be, and cannibalize those you need to for space parts."

"Fix them ourselves?"

"You three, meet me at my place and we'll figure it out," once I hack the main computer to get the damned things schematics, I told myself. "Oh, and I want all you guys complaining about how hard you're working to keep to schedule. But never mention what we're doing to keep up."

"You're not being paranoid, are you?"

"No, this reeks of Chip and his friends… If it's someone else, it doesn't matter; let them think this sabotage is working."

"Whatever you say, Boss."

"And figure there'll be some other surprises—and we get bonus credits for keeping to schedule…"

I decided it wasn't the best idea to walk home alone after Sarge complimented me on my shift's continuing to meet schedule. Well, that and the fact I was drawing dark looks from grubbers working other shifts.

My now unofficial bodyguard, Benny, reported for the next shift with a black eye after that. "You all right?"

"You should see the other guys," he replied, grimly.

"Really?"

"I made friends with the local Fabricator gang, I mean, who have taken to policing their section… They broke up the fight after I laid two of them out."

I grinned. "Check the fabber, my friend, then get back on the line."

"Sure, Boss."

At the end of the shift I found myself being walked home by half my team. It turned out I might have been smarter bringing all of them. Chip's entire crew was waiting for us.

"Well, Kid, heard your boys are Top Shift again this week," he said.

"Work hard and you could make Top Shift next week," I replied, wondering why Sarge never felt compelled to share that detail with us.

"I'm tired of being compared to a little shit like you."

Oh, that explained it, I thought. *Thank you, Colonial Management for being so helpful in fostering the competitive spirit.*

Chip gestured. "Come on, you and I— right here, right now."

I swallowed, glancing at his grinning companions. *Okay, this was going to hurt.* I took a step forward only to hear a voice I wasn't expecting say, "Chip, don't be an ass."

I turned and realized my friends and I weren't outnumbered any more.

"Cindy, come to fight your man's battles for him, eh?"

"Thomas, home— now!"

"Reg!" Name after name… Chip's friends went home with their ladies, who looked less than pleased at their behavior.

"Millie, you're embarrassing me!" one guy said, as his wife took him by the ear, cradling her sleeping baby in her other arm.

Chip stared about him. I briefly wondered where Lisa was, then thought it best not to remark on her absence. Perhaps it would spare her the beating I was apparently not going to suffer. "This isn't over, Grime."

I swallowed as my wife came up next to me and shouted after him, "Grow up, Chip!"

Sarge and the other Elders called a Grubbers' Council Meeting. "Well, boys and girls, our job is almost done training you and your fellow colonists… Of the six Grubber shifts two have really stood out. Chip, your group has done something we rarely see. Your group has managed to exceed our expectations, earning a substantial bonus. We've seen teams work hard, competing to be the best, but you have taken it to another level completely… Grime, your group has maintained its schedule although there have been more reports of damaged sonic shovels than recorded in years. You may not realize it, but the team after yours has constantly complained about every aspect of your shift's work, which has resulted in their struggling to maintain the schedule, which has forced the other shifts to work twice as hard."

I grimaced, as Chip and his friends grinned.

"Throughout our time here we have conducted inspections and reviews of all grubber activities and found that your crew, Grime, is apparently taking dangerous shortcuts just to maintain your schedule. Maintaining that schedule has earned your people a bonus, which would seem to be totally undeserved.

"Our investigation is now complete." Sarge shook his head, then said angrily, "Acting like children is going to get you all killed. Your lives depend on hard—honest—work. To make this crystal clear, we are rescinding our previous bonus decisions. Something we have only had to do at one other colony, a colony that actually failed to sustain itself faster than any we have ever seen, leading to the deaths of nearly every man, woman, and child… In other words, they succeeded in killing each other. Oh, and this led to your colony being settled here after we had to come in a fix the mess they left."

I winced and knew I wasn't the only one who felt the words as a physical blow.

"So, Chip, congratulations, we have rescinded your team's bonuses and decided to double Grime's shift's. Chip's shift is docked one year of credit for their ongoing acts of sabotage. And, no, Grime's people never ratted you out.

"We have hidden monitors throughout the colony… You're free to hunt them down after we leave. It should provide you hours and hours of fun before you lot get another chance to get everyone around you killed."

That comment was greeted by stunned looks.

"Oh, we've notified the other Districts, so they know whose intent on killing them, too… as part of our recommendation that they leave you demoted to Junior Grubber for the rest of your life… as brief as it'll likely be."

He pointed at the main monitor, "Mr. Barret," he said, glaring at third shift's leader, "you are hereby docked two years credit and we've demoted you from Boss with the same recommendation to your Colony leadership. Based on the bribes you have already been paid, you likely won't miss it.

"Grime, congratulation, we're promoting you to Head Grubber." He handed me a rock of all things. "And this is to commemorate the occasion. This is Deimos."

"Uh, thanks, Sarge, I'll, um, cherish it."

"Do that, and think of it as one of the rocks that hangs over you and this colony… Oh, and work out your little problems before you all get yourselves killed… because this foolishness will get everyone of you killed, otherwise…" He looked around, "and, people, understand, Grime's a miracle and I recommend you look to his people to supervise and retrain anyone who isn't meeting expectations."

I came home with more bodyguards. A gang with Fabricator patches on their pressure suited arms, which I supposed didn't make a bad badge of honor, were now policing our sector as well. "Congrats on the promotion, Grime," the Fabricator team leader said.

"Uh, thanks… I think," I muttered, knowing Benny, who had been more upbeat about approaching the Fabricator gang for help, a gang they were, suggested he had experience in understanding gangs.

"Thanks, Julio," Benny said.

"Glad to keep the peace, just like on the streets back home… We have enough problems to deal with. Our babies are counting on us not to screw this up…"

Lots of babies and their parents, who were little more than kids themselves, I thought.

I went through the hatch into my apartment, feeling light headed suddenly. Cindy glanced at me and frowned. "How was your day?"

I set Deimos down on the table. "I've been promoted—and Chip got what was coming to him." I sat down on what I'd come to think of as my chair and saw fish swimming by through the transparent conduit.

"Somehow, I doubt that," she said sarcastically. "I take it this gang that's expanding into our territory was your doing?"

"What can I say? I make friends everywhere."

"You bribed them?"

"Not exactly… More, trading favors for mutual benefit."

The babies began crying. I went over to the crib and picked up our son as Cindy came over and picked up our daughter.

As I soothed my little boy, I told Cindy, "So, I'm officially Head Grubber. Chip was demoted and his crew got docked."

"Holy…" she said, rocking our daughter. "Gary, can't you stay out of trouble? There's only so much the ladies can do."

"Not according to my good old Dad."

"You know Chip's going to kill you."

"Oh, I expect he'll try. But he doesn't know me very well… I'm a survivor—and a lot smarter than him."

She looked at me with that inscrutable way of hers. I smiled, my stomach in knots, looking at little Deimos laying there on the table, knowing it was a message from the Elders and added, "Isn't life on Mars grand?"

Chapter 9 – Six Feet Under on Mars

Believe me, you do not want to wake hearing the words I awoke to: "He's alive."

I groaned, feeling awful. "Wha – what happened?"

Sin was staring at me in shock from the curtain to our bedroom, her eyes wide as the twins cried. I blinked, realizing someone was nestled beside me on the bed, "Huh?"

"Definitely tracking," Lisa muttered.

"Thank Heavens," Sin said, hurrying to my side.

Realizing I could barely move, I turned to see Lisa beside me, "What are you doing?"

Frowning, "Helping keep you warm and, well, holding you down."

"Holding me down?"

Lisa sighed, "And I was trying to get some sleep. It's not like we can control the temperature much."

"We've practically had to sit on you at times," Sin said, "to prevent you from making things any worse."

I tried to lift my head, "What?"

"Lisa's been nursing you," Sin said as Lisa carefully sat up.

"We've splinted your broken legs, and your left arm, too," Lisa added.

I frowned, realizing it had to be more than that. "Why do I feel like I'm tied up?"

"We bound your ribs also," Sin answered. "A number are fractured, some may be broken."

"Uh, huh. That… that explains why I… why I feel a bit out of breath."

"You're lucky not to have punctured a lung," Lisa said.

Sin frowned, nodding.

Lisa dabbed a damp cloth to my forehead. "Promise not to try to move much. At least without my help."

"Fine."

"Promise," Lisa said.

"I promise," I sighed, knowing how much worse this was that it felt.

Lisa slipped from under the covers as Sin said, "Look at me, Gary. Do you remember what happened?"

"Remember?"

"Gary, do you remember the accident?"

"Accident?" I frowned, trying to turn my head.

Sin took my face in her hands and looked me in the eyes. "Gary, think… What's the last thing you remember?"

Puzzled, I thought back. "I—I was on my shift… Someone came running—someone wearing a pressure suit…" I blinked, remembering, "Lisa…"

"That's right," Lisa said, lowering her head. "I had to warn you."

"You were shouting for me to get everyone… clear."

"That's good, Gary," Sin said, meeting Lisa's gaze. "Very good."

"Lisa, you could have gotten yourself killed," I muttered. "A pressure suit can't last in there long."

She looked away. "I figured that."

"She did well enough," Sin said. "And, honestly, I couldn't exactly deal with you and the twins alone, now could I?"

"What… what happened?"

Lisa wiped tears from her cheeks, then laid down against me, making me twinge from the pain, nestling her face against mine, sobbing. "I'm sorry, Gary. So, sorry…"

I closed my eyes, wondering what she was talking about.

Let's see, I was Head Grubber and still dealing with dissent in the ranks from the demoted… I opened my eyes and looked at Sin, looking at me worriedly. She had the most beautiful eyes.

Lisa came shouting warning… I shut my eyes. "How long ago—"

"Gary," Sin shook her head as Lisa sobbed the louder, "it's been nearly two weeks since that shift."

"Two… weeks?"

Lisa kissed my cheek, "Twelve days. You wouldn't leave without the last of your team… The emergency crew only found you—"

"Because Lisa wouldn't leave," Sin said, "though, you sent her to the lock… She knew where you were."

I blinked, "Lisa… you knew."

Her arm across me tightened. She was very quiet, my cheeks wet with her tears and those of my shock and anger.

"How many did… did I lose?

"Gary," Sin whispered.

"How many?" I demanded.

"Six," Lisa whispered.

Being Head Grubber didn't mean my team didn't have a shift. A number of my former teammates were now in charge of the two teams I had split up. I'd hoped breaking them up would dilute their anger at being demoted and help them rebuild their credits by working with more successful teams.

I guess even doing that wasn't enough to blunt Chip's ability to seek revenge. I remember supervising and being about an hour into our shift when my display noted the lock cycling. "Booby trap!" someone yelled, in the loping run so many were adopting.

"What?" I think I said, believing I'd misheard, realizing they wore only a standard pressure suit.

"Booby trap! Get everyone out!"

I knew that voice, recognized the slight figure in that pressure suit with its small oxygen tank. Lisa. I shouted, "Alert! Clear the area! Everyone back to the hatch! Especially you!" I ordered her, remembering ordering her.

Not as much as the explosion, I suddenly remembered as if a sonic regulator were somehow embedded in the one of the walls as dirt and rock spewed and a pressure wave brought down the ceiling.

I was lucky to be alive...

Lisa sobbed, "If I'd only known sooner."

I winced in pain. "Um... How..."

Sin cleared her throat, "Uh, Lisa, it's all right. He doesn't blame you."

She stopped, looked up and blinked, "Oh... I'm, uh, hurting you."

I blinked. "How?"

Lisa leaned back, "Chip... Chip came home looking like the proverbial cat that ate the canary... and he was drunk..."

"He hurt you?" I muttered.

"I—I managed to grab my pressure suit and get out of the apartment. He yelled from the hatch, 'You've nowhere to go—and Cindy's going to be no better off after this shift!' That's when I knew..."

"How—how am I even still alive?"

Sin shook her head, "That damned database of yours... Why didn't you tell me it had an emergency medical section?"

"Good thing you have it," Lisa said almost breathless, looking at me as if she wanted to say something else. "Cindy couldn't tell me how you came by it."

I blinked, glancing at Sin, "Huh, did I forget to mention that?"

"Just like the medical section."

I nodded, trying to ignore the pain.

"Lisa, no time for a lot of questions… And, you, hubby dear, will be delighted to know that the Elders sent a rather brief message after the accident, which has made far too many people curious as to the state of your health."

"Huh?"

"They said we wouldn't hear from them again until a grown-up was in charge over here… and they said if you died, they expected the colony was likely going to have to be written off."

My eyes felt heavy and I must have drifted off to sleep.

"Gary, are you thirsty?" Sin asked when I next woke.

I licked my lips.

"I'll get you some water," Lisa said, wiping her tears and scurrying off the bed, knocking something off, which hit the floor.

I mouthed to Sin, "Thanks."

She whispered, "You owe me big," picking up what fell. It was Deimos.

I frowned, eyes widening, "Owe… The debt to Colonial Management?"

"I improvised, so we're not in as much debt as we could be… if that even matters now. Like this rock, huh, which is now, apparently, chipped."

I frowned as she set it down back beside my good hand on the bed. "Story of my life… Now, what?"

"Now, that's the question, isn't it?" Sin sighed.

Lisa hurried back with a bulb of water. She tilted my head up. I winced, seeing stars. "Oh, sorry."

"Don't cry," I muttered.

"Really, Lisa, you have to stop crying," Sin said.

"What are you doing here, Lisa?"

"Oh, besides nursing you… You owe her your life," Sin said, when Lisa looked away. "And Chip knows it."

"So, you're safer here," I whispered, dizzy.

Lisa nodded, eyes wide, "Much safer. He knows I could testify against him… and he'd kill me if he could."

"I'm surprised Chip hasn't stopped by to finish the job," I sighed, closing my eyes.

"Well, he's not very popular at the moment," Sin smiled.

"And she told him spouses can't testify—and that I'm pregnant," Lisa admitted.

"You're pregnant?"

Lisa blinked, "Um, uh, huh."

Frowning, I glanced at Sin, "You lied to him."

"I told him you were in a coma and unlikely to live. You mind me lying to him about that?"

"Not in the least," I replied.

Sin went back through the curtain as the babies cried. "Mommy's coming."

"Gary," Lisa said, squeezing the bulb, sending cool water into my mouth. I drank. "We can't let anyone know you're awake. Best everyone thinks you're dying, while you heal up."

I met her gaze. "There's more to this."

"Chip claims he had nothing to do with it. No one believes it… But, well, he's unofficially Head Grubber and controls an entire section of the District."

"Oh, that's wonderful…" I frowned. "So who's in control of the rest of the District?"

Lisa shook her head, "Um, you sort of are."

I blinked. "I am?"

"Well, Cindy is— in your name…"

"Sin?"

"Yes, Gary," she replied, too sweetly, as the twins stopped crying.

"Sin… Exactly how are we in charge of most of the District?"

"Oh, that? It just sort of happened… Your team moved everyone else out of the corridor, and took over along with some, uh, friends, who've moved into the other apartments… Oh, and they are armed with those sonic shovel things."

I blinked. "Armed?"

"Benny made sure they came back with the damned things. Chip has some, too. Apparently, all that were in for repair and what spare components he could liberate."

"They work in atmosphere?"

"Pretty damned well," Sin smiled, a wicked gleam in her eye.

Lisa chuckled, "Before Chip got any of theirs working, Benny fired a blast at Chip, which knocked him on his ass."

"He didn't."

"He told me it wasn't set to max and shouldn't bring down the place on us before I ever told him to fire."

I grinned, sorry I'd missed that.

Lisa offered me another squirt of water.

I frowned.

She blinked. "Uh, the pain bad?"

"No," I lied, frowning, thoughts whirling. "Sin, the Council must be doing something."

"They are. They're discussing what to do… about everything—every damned day."

I winced. "Wonderful."

Playing the man in a coma under the circumstances was easier than I thought. Sin was playing hostess to a number of very important guests, or perhaps you could call it an infant playdate. The apartment was not exactly built for such a number, but it was not like we had any better choice.

Listening to every word and baby cry, eyes closed,

I decided it sounded more like Sin was holding Court. "Thank you for meeting with us, Mrs. Grime. Here's a little gift we hope might make, well, life a little better for you."

"It's a tea blend from the one of the farm sections," another voice added, pleasantly.

"Tea… real tea?" Sin sounded choked up by the gift and I could understand why. Tea was a luxury I doubt anyone back home could afford.

"I'm sorry I wasn't able to borrow more chairs," Sin said.

"We completely understand… We're a bit larger delegation than you had any right to expect," one of the women said.

I heard someone opening the curtain seal and a baby coo. "Well, he's definitely breathing."

"Leave him be," Lisa said, rushing over, the sound of the plastic being resealed shut grating on my ears.

"Can't fault a gal for verifying the guy's not a corpse."

Sin said, "You could have asked nicely. It's not like I didn't invite you here for a reason."

"We agreed to meet here because you're safer here than anywhere."

"Well, there's that," Sin admitted as I struggled not to smile.

"And as long as he's alive, you've the Golden Goose."

Huh?

"What do you mean?"

"You haven't checked your account?"

"Of course, I have, Helen… He's being laid up is costing us."

"Nowhere near as much as it should. They've increased the value of what he's donated to the Colonial Gene Bank."

Sin chuckled. "Really? That's… well, I guess the

Elders are making a statement."

"Colonial Management certainly has. They set the values, after all… So, as long as he's, well, capable…"

"Helen, isn't it enough she knows she has some resources under the circumstances?"

"Fine, Maggie, enough said… But at least Colonial Management's, apparently, still communicating, if obliquely."

"Cindy, we checked, and, well, certain other individuals here in your district, you'll be unsurprised to know, have been revalued by the Gene Bank, too."

"Also a good number substantially devalued."

"To near worthlessness."

Oh, boy.

It sounded like there was a collective "ah" and chuckles. "The silver lining, Mrs. Grime."

"Please, call me Cindy."

"Thank you, Cindy."

"But what your saying is Colonial Management is playing us off each other, you mean," Sin said.

"There's that," I thought it was Helen said.

"And the Council's stuck in endless debate, trying to keep the colony running… and not doing a great job of it," Sin said.

There was silence.

"I've been watching the comm," Sin said. "This District isn't the only one with problems…"

Only the babies could heard.

"Mrs.—Cindy… We've another reason that we wanted to meet with you here… How is it this apartment is not monitored?"

"Monitored?" Sin half protested.

"How did you get this apartment off-line? The Elders wired the entire colony—and from Central they could see every apartment—as Central still can, except, well, this apartment and some others in this District."

"Sin wisely pretended innocence. "Really? How

odd…"

"How did you get this room off the grid?" Helen asked.

"I've really no idea what you're talking about."

"How do we get our apartments off the spy-eye grid?"

Oh, my.

There was silence, Lisa squealed, "You mean they could see everything?"

Sin replied, "Well, the Elders were pretty truthful about keeping an eye on us… and saying we should have fun ridding ourselves of such things."

"All of which Central should still have access to… a 'parting gift' is what they told Council."

"Really," Sin said, I bet doing her best not to glance in my direction.

Oh, Benny, you took "watching each other's backs" to a whole other level.

"So, Mrs. Grime… how do we do the same?"

"Well, now, that's quite the favor to ask…" Sin replied, which was followed by silence, save from the babies, who their mothers soothed. *Ah, Sin was in her element… These ladies were going to pay dearly.*

Lisa checked on me, whispering in my ear, "You're doing really well… Just a little longer."

I think I imagined her kissing me on the cheek before leaving my side.

"We agreed then?" Sin asked.

A hesitant voice, sounding a bit aggrieved, "Agreed."

"Good, in that case, I'll send someone to show you how."

Our guests soon left. I opened my eyes, hearing Sin pulling apart the curtain seals, "Gary, how did you manage it?"

"Manage what?"

"Out with it. It's one thing to disable the spy-eye in here."

I smiled. "You've made quite a bargain."

"Somehow I think you have, too."

"Well," I smiled at her, then relented at her glare. "I felt I owed Benny his privacy."

"Only him?"

"Well, you know, my other bodyguards deserved their privacy, too."

"Who knows how to do it?"

"Well, Benny is pretty observant, which I suspect is why Julio and his gang became our friends, too… That hasn't changed, has it?"

"No, the gang's come in real handy, though, Benny's not shared any regulators with them… Now, what do you think he'll want in exchange for helping our recent guests?"

"For you joining the Council?"

"I'm not joining the Council."

"No, you're joining the Cabal that is actually the Council, which just visited."

"Now, Gary…" Sin replied.

Lisa was staring wide-eyed.

"Oh, don't, 'now Gary me'… So, what were they talking about earlier about me being the Golden Goose?"

Lisa coughed and coughed.

"Oh, Lisa, come, here's a bulb of water."

"Sin?" I said.

Lisa kept coughing, bulb now in hand.

Chapter 10 – Waste Not, Want Not

A subsequent sudden meeting of only two members of the Cabal followed Benny's visiting each of the ladies' homes while their hubbies endlessly debated, which worried Sin as much as me since we barely got any warning. Hurriedly pretending I was in a coma, I focused on keeping my breath steady. I listened as our guests presented Sin a fresh fruit basket of all things.

To hear Benny tell it when he completed his circuit of visits, the ladies had expressed their personal gratitude to a more personal degree. One they never would have with the spy-eyes still active.

"Cindy, we've lost hydroponics in Districts Six, Sixteen, and now Twenty-six, which makes the gift we brought you all the more precious," said Helen Chou, who represented District One, her baby making a whimpering sound. "Worse, Waste Management has, well, shut down, which is not good for anyone."

"And you're telling me this, why?"

There was a pause. "Cindy, the babies are getting real sick in those districts."

At first I wasn't sure if one of our twins began to cry or one of our guests as if to punctuate that until Sin said, "Oh, Mommy's not forgotten you. Sorry for the interruption."

"Uh, not a problem," the other woman continued. "Fact is, their families are abandoning their homes— and the neighboring districts don't want them, so they're crowding into whatever communal areas they can."

"It's a literal mess, Cindy," Helen said.

"Are you seeking to relocate them here?" Sin asked.

"No," Helen replied. "The problem is that the septic system is backed up, according to Gregory…"

"He says there's a blockage somewhere."

"A blockage, Maggie?" Sin said. "That sounds like something your husband's in charge of—"

"You'd think Gregory and his people could fix that," Helen sighed.

"There must be something like a plunger," Lisa offered.

There was an awkward silence as they, apparently, stared at Lisa.

"Of course, there is," Maggie replied, exasperated, "but the fools there never really learned how to access the manual. They just followed the trainers around and didn't ask enough questions before they left, reminding them that they really ought to do their homework."

"You've got to be kidding," Sin muttered.

"Believe me, those assigned to Waste Management didn't want the job, and figured someone else could fix the mess..." Maggie said.

"Colonial Management's been rather serious about not talking to Central," Helen replied, "and telling us what to do."

"But there must be a manual," Lisa said.

There was silence; even the babies didn't make a sound.

I frowned as Sin said, "Well, Lisa's right. There must be one."

"Believe me, Gregory's been looking in the vid system... but even he can't find it. And, he's considered the Waste Management's genius."

Who apparently didn't read the manual, either, I thought. *Genius, right.*

"Well, he best find it or more than just three districts are going to be effected," Sin said.

"He knows, believe me, he knows," Maggie said.

"Only thing the Council can agree on, with thousands looking for working port-a-potties, is that someone had better find that manual." Helen admitted.

"They say it should be on the system. But they can't find it…"

Sin said, "And you're sharing this with me, because…"

"We're desperate for help. Helen and I thought… well, you knew how to deal with the spy-eyes. Can you help us with this?" Maggie said, sounding desperate.

"Oh, hmm, I may have," Sin said, "an inquisitive friend, who might be of help finding it… But my friend doesn't like doing things for free."

"What'll it cost us?"

"A favor at the very least…" she replied. "A big one."

"Waste Management will owe a big one for that manual."

"Hmm, somehow, I don't think my friend will want a favor from those guys."

"No, I don't suppose anyone will once the system works," she replied.

There were appreciative chuckles.

"Well, we'll owe you a big favor, if your friend can help us."

"Gregory will be good for it," his wife said. "He can do something useful for the Council and the entire colony for once."

"That's all I ask," Sin said.

As soon as the ladies and their babies left, Lisa helped me sit up as Sin cradled our daughter and went to the vid. She entered my name and password on the menu. "Sin, I never told you my password."

"No, you didn't," she said. "But it's a good thing I watched you using it—you being Head Grubber with better access and all."

"It's not like the Council doesn't have at least as good access, Sin."

She tapped the screen. Kept searching and calling

up more menus.

"It's got to be here," she muttered in frustration as the baby grew fussier, his twin stirring in her crib. Sin turned around, "Gary, do something!"

"Do something?"

Lisa glanced at the crib.

"Help me get to the vid…"

"What?" Lisa said.

Sin nodded, "Leave the twins to me… Help him."

Shaking her head, murmuring this was crazy, Lisa spread the plastic curtain wide, then came back to me and helped me rise. Every step agony, Lisa was my crutch, shoring me up, my broken arm across her shoulders. "Lean me up against the wall," I grimaced, Lisa looking up at me as we both struggled to cross the room.

Pain shooting up my legs, I tapped the vid screen. Calling up internal menus, looking for any way via back door to any of the other systems.

"Well?"

"Sin, I'm not seeing any way to access other resource system info."

"There has to be."

"In Central, I'm sure… from here?"

"Keep looking."

Lisa half-glanced over her shoulder as we swayed, "Cindy, he can barely stand."

"Gary, ignore the pain and find that Waste Management manual!"

Eyes half lidded, I started over in the menu and called up the maintenance info on our port-a-potties. Tapped, "Repair."

'WHAT IS THE NATURE OF THE NEEDED REPAIR?'

"Blockage."

A schematic of how to fix a line blockage came up.

'DID THIS CORRECT THE ISSUE? YES/NO.'

"No," I tapped.

It offered another option.

'DID THIS CORRECT THE ISSUE? YES/NO.'

"No," I tapped.

It offered other options all of which I told the system did not correct the problem.

'PLEASE SPECIFY THE ISSUE FURTHER.'

"The entire waste system for the District is blocked," I tapped out on the screen, the pain shooting up my legs, becoming unbearable.

The screen began to flash. Then something flashed on the screen. 'GRIME, NOT DEAD YET? OR THIS THE MRS. USING GRIME'S CODE?'

Lisa gasped, "Cindy!"

"Hi, Sarge," I tapped out, the motion adding to the shooting pain. "I could use the manual for Waste Management before I have to deal with even more crap."

'WELL, GRIME, SMART AS EVER... LET'S SEE IF YOU CAN KEEP FAMILY AND FRIENDS ALIVE A LITTLE LONGER, BUT YOU DIDN'T GET THIS FROM ME.'

At least that's what I thought it said before collapsing, unconscious.

I woke feeling like lightning was coursing through me and moaned. Lisa, one of the twins in her arms sitting on the bed beside me, set a hand across my mouth.

A familiar man's voice said, "I don't even know how you managed to call that up—but you want me to what?"

"Benny, I just need you to go there and use your sonic regulator to blast out the blockage."

"You're crazy..."

"The manual recommends this in an emergency...

and, believe me, this is an emergency."

"Blasting the blockage—you have any idea what that'll do?" Benny demanded.

"Babies are sick and it won't be long before everyone else will be, too."

"Ms. Cindy…"

"Benny, one sonic regulator."

"Could do more than blowing us to… uh, you get the idea."

"Believe me, I know… but just giving the Wasters access to that manual and schematic showing the blockage isn't going to fix the problem… not without a Grubber's help at this point."

"I don't dare take a regulator out of the District," Benny said.

"I know you're afraid that Chip will make his play," Sin replied.

"Benny's right, Cindy. Chip wants Gary and—" Lisa hesitated.

Benny finished for her. "He wants Gary dead. I figure he's five Grubber's Best Friends that would have been in the repair shop with every spare part… spare parts we don't have for those the boys managed to bring out with us."

"Benny," Sin said, "I trust you, and your friends out there, to keep us alive."

"Ms. Cindy, if I'm not here, I don't know you can trust all of them."

"What'll it take to, uh, cement that trust?"

Benny was silent.

"Our team will do everything they can to keep Gary alive… but the others, well, they don't owe him their lives, and know him like we do."

I bit Lisa's hand. "Ow!"

"BENNY!" I yelled.

"Gary?"

"You know how crazy this is," Benny said.

"Lisa, you know Chip better than anyone," I said from my prone position, looking up at the ceiling.

She gently bounced my son in her arms and answered, "The second he hears that Benny's left the district with some guards… he'll come after us."

"So, that part of the plan should work like a charm," Sin said, shaking her head, standing off to the left, cradling our daughter. "Gary, it's just the staying alive part after that I'm having trouble with."

"What? Because I'm flat on my back, you don't believe I can out think that bastard?"

Sin replied, "He is the one that literally brought part of the warren down on you."

"But we didn't have the computer access, which is a lot more than we thought."

"The access that the Elders can cut as quickly as they provided it," Sin reminded him.

"And you could offer that to the Council…" Benny said, suggesting it yet again.

"Benny, what good would that really do?" Gary replied. "Best to just transfer the schematic of the waste recycling system and where the blockage is to your vac suit and have you repair that problem."

"Which means me walking across the friggin' colony, then…" Benny paused, "explaining to them that one of our friends has hacked the colony's restricted database and I can repair the blockage."

"You want to trust them with that access," I asked, "when Colonial Management hasn't for some reason?"

"And the Council's shown so much leadership already," Sin said.

Benny shook his head. "Yet you've access, and the best you've come up with is this mad plan to deal with Chip once and for all."

I held Deimos beneath my good hand, a tad lighter. "Oh, I think things will work out just fine."

"We can make this work," Lisa said, trying to

sound like she believed it.

"Fine, Boss, I'll do my part… but if you get yourselves killed, don't say I didn't warn you."

Sin looked at Lisa. "Turn around."

Lisa did. "This will never work."

"Even with that little bit of padding, you still look too—"

"Scrawny?" Lisa sighed.

"Thin was what I was about to say," she replied.

"We'll never convince him I'm pregnant."

I sat on the bed, feeling shaky, "You're right, we need to modify the plan a bit… And we don't need him to be certain Lisa's pregnant. But anything that might make him wonder is all to the good."

"He'll never believe it…" Lisa sighed.

I winced. Nothing for it but to make myself an even more important target of his ire. "Oh, yes, he will."

Lisa blinked, "Huh?"

"Forget the padding… We'll need to hide you— and all I need to do is laugh at him about it."

Frowning, Sin muttered, "Huh? That might just work." She looked at me. "But more effective coming from me than you, Gary."

"Uh, Sin, leave that to me," I replied, hoping I sound confident.

"Gary, I'll handle that part. Though, I don't think that's going to stop him from trying to kill all of us in the least."

"He'll try, but it's not going to work," I said, hoping I was right.

"Gary, everything depends on this plan working," she replied.

I smiled, holding up Deimos, "Worse come to worse, I'll use this."

"Throwing a rock at him," Lisa sighed. "Hope

you've good aim in this gravity."

"Oh, aim won't have anything to do it," I smiled.

"You're betting all our lives, Gary," Sin said.

"Trust me, I'm betting the entire colony… We can't let the Chip, or Council, play games with our lives… The Elders were dead serious about everything they told us. And, though, they didn't tell us everything we need to know, I think they've very good reasons for having done so."

Lisa frowned. "Well, there must be more we can do."

I looked around. "Huh… Maybe there is… Lisa—"

Her eyes lit as she was more than happy to do as I suggested.

Sin canted her head, "Now that that's settled. I'd like to ask you something… How long ago do you think this colony was first established?"

"Uh, it bothers you this place is rather big."

"And this apartment isn't new…"

"Fine, according to my database and based on the tech around us, I'd say about forty years or so."

"That long…"

I nodded. "We definitely aren't the first colony to settle here. Each must have expanded the place before…"

Sin nodded as Lisa set up preparing our little surprise.

"For the next wave of immigrants," I finished instead.

Lisa finished and came back and sat on the edge of the bed, "You really think this will work?"

I lied, smiling, "Definitely."

Part Three: Nothing Goes to Waste on Mars
Chapter 11 – Life Can be Shitty

Sin tapped the pad and the hatch opened. I recognized the voice of one of my Grubbers, "Trouble. We're going to check it out."

The hatch closed.

I turned and looked at her.

"Well, this is it, then," Sin said. "Be good and play dead to the world."

I sighed. This was the part I hated most. The only good thing was that we'd agreed that this throw of the dice play was too dangerous for the twins to be caught up in, so their pods were now with those we knew we could trust.

It didn't take long to buzz.

The vid activated and I heard Chip say, "Hi, Sin. Thought I'd stop by and see how you folks are doing." He pointed the sonic regulator he carried at the frame. "You have until the count of three to let me in… One… two—"

The hatch immediately opened. "Hi, Chip," Sin said, "what a surprise to see you."

He ignored her, looking around the room, "Where is she?"

"You mean Lisa? She's not home right now. She's having a pregnancy med-visit with her midwife."

"Oh, come off it. The kid's not pregnant… not for the lack of us trying, understand?"

Sin replied coldly, "Is that what you call it? Well, for a man who felt his virility questioned, you should be happy she's going to have your baby… Then, again, we both know you're really here to kill her."

He didn't answer that, merely directed Sin to move toward the bedroom area. "Gary, playing possum or he really still in a coma over there?"

"You nearly killed him, Chip," Sin responded.

"I did no such thing."

"Oh, really? Then why are you here aiming that thing at me?"

"You know there's a rumor that you've managed to get this apartment off-line, great scam if anyone believes that."

"Really? Well, I like my privacy—from the Elders and anyone else who has no right to be spying on me and mine. But you know that, you've your own reasons to make sure no one sees what you've been doing…

"So you've knocked out the cameras out there and know no one knows you're here or there's any chance you might confess on camera," I heard her say, then chuckle.

"All I'm doing is seeking to defend myself from those I know to be the most subversive elements in this district."

"Subversive?" Sin laughed as I struggled to play dead to the world.

"Gary's friends stole regulators after that terrible accident and took over most of the district—if my friends and I hadn't raided the repair bay for this one and the others, well, who knows what you'd have done," I could hear his smile.

"Hadn't you stolen them before the unexplained sonic explosion that killed six people and nearly did in Gary, too?"

"That was an accident, not a sonic explosion. Under a better team I'm sure that would never have happened at all."

"You know, it does seem to me to have been well timed."

"As well timed as you and I being matched and paired at the émigré center in Death Valley?"

Voice cold, "You mean the day you almost lost us both our chances to go to Mars?"

"Me? They said we were perfect for each other."

"They were so wrong."

"No, they weren't, and you know it… Both of us are made to rule. Oh, I know about you and the Council of Ladies. Scheming behind the dithering Council's backs, that's so you. Poor, Gary-boy, he gets a beautiful baby who'll do anything to get what she wants." He chuckled. "Even if it kills him… I've no doubt trying to impress you is what caused that accident."

I didn't need to see her face in that moment. I knew she was glaring back at him.

"Well, now's the time to do the smart thing and make things right. You can join me. I'll take you in and we'll make beautiful babies together."

"Go to Hell, Chip."

He laughed, "We're already here, babe. And, face it, this district is mine as of this moment… You can join me or find yourself living in the Commons with all those pathetic folk from District Twenty-Six."

"You're such a fool."

He reached over, one handed, and tore open the plastic curtain. "Wakey, wakey, Gary Grime."

I opened my eyes, turned my head, yawning, "Oh, I bet you were hoping to wake me with a kiss."

"Actually," he trained the regulator on me and pulled the trigger.

"NO!" Cindy cried.

Click.

"Hmm," I smiled, "you did recharge it fully before coming here, didn't you?"

He stared at the control gauge as Sin stared at me.

Slapping the side of the regulator, Chip muttered, "What?"

"You really should have paid more attention," I said, trying to get a better view of him; leveraging myself up on my good elbow.

He rushed forward moving to shove me, and tripped over the thin wire we'd laid out to greet him. Down he went, going thud against the bed frame.

"You all right?"

Chip laid his hands to the side of my bed to pick himself up. I slammed my splinted arm down on his fingers.

"Ow!"

The pain of doing that made me almost black out. Lisa scurried around from behind the bed and grabbed up his regulator and ran with it to Sin.

"Hey! Give that back, you little—!"

Sin grabbed it from Lisa and aimed it at him. "Now, Chip, watch your language—and, Gary, if you'd be so kind as to turn this back on."

There was a sudden humming noise. I held up the remote that Sarge had given me when I was promoted, normally hidden inside little Deimos.

Chip's eyes widened. "What?"

"Well, I am Head Grubber and the position came with this really nice toy," I admitted, though, not until I'd dropped it, thinking I'd broken the little moon to find it. Before he could get any ideas, I tossed the remote over to Lisa, who caught it.

Chip stared, gaze narrowing.

"You know, Sarge and the Elders apparently had safeguards in case, well, anyone got any ideas about using the regulators against them."

Sin smiled, nodding toward the vid. "Smile for the camera, Chip. After all, everyone in Central's watching and knows you came here to kill Gary and your wife… oh, and likely me, just for spite."

"Lisa's a worthless little shit. Just like you!"

"No, you are!" Lisa yelled, face flush with anger.

"You really should be more respectful. Lisa's your wife, and pregnant, Chip," I said.

"Oh, don't give me that. She's not pregnant… and

look who she ran to the second she dared try… You, Grime."

Lisa said, "I ran here because they're good people! And, I am pregnant, you arrogant worthless… worthless…" she gasped.

"Lisa, we get the point," I said, thinking it a bit funny she couldn't bring herself to say a bad word.

"Chip, you've lost this play," Sin said. "Now, you've the choice of walking out an airlock without a suit and dancing in Hell out there—or go find another district that might be willing to take in such a…" she looked at Lisa, "swell guy like you."

"Lost this play?" Chip laughed. "You know, I didn't come alone… and you didn't think you could exactly hide the twins, now, did you?"

"No," I said, "we definitely didn't think you'd come alone… You're too much of a coward, who would definitely send your friends after defenseless babies."

He frowned.

There was a buzz. The vid screen suddenly showed a view of two Grubbers with sonic regulators. "Boss Man, Boss Lady, we got all of 'em. They went for the bait just like you said they would."

Sin nodded to Lisa, who tapped the hatch access pad. The hatch opened. "Excellent. Chip, I'm sure those friends of yours will be happy to go out the airlock with you…"

"I'm sure they'll watch your back—like my teammates have—for me and mine," I offered.

The vid suddenly showed the watching Council. "Head Grubber Grime, we concur with your assessment that this gentlemen no longer be allowed to reside in your district—and wish him well living on the surface for the rest of eternity."

"You lot need me! He's crippled!" Chip shouted.

"He's done more for this colony than you can

imagine," the Head of the Council said, who could not be more than eighteen or nineteen. "Mr. Grime, thank you for finding and providing the solution to the main blockage to the waste system. You colleague has successfully cleared it. The system's warning lights are only showing yellow alert now. Your friend should have the secondary issues cleared in the next hour or so…"

Which couldn't be too soon for Benny, who we all owed big time for this.

"And the copy of the system manual you found for my people, Mr. Grime," another of the Council members said, "will help us keep it operating properly. We're studying it—as if our lives depended on it… We owe you a debt that will be difficult to repay."

I looked at the vid and was about to say, "Think nothing of it," when Sin said, "Well, perhaps, we should call in on part of that debt and help Councilor Gregory a bit more…"

Everyone on the screen gave her their full attention. She certainly had mine as this wasn't part of the plan.

"I'd like to ask for leniency for Chip here and his friends—" Sin said, "that is, if they'd prefer not to take a permanent trip to the surface."

Chip was staring at her as the guards bound his wrists.

"I think they could really make themselves useful shoveling the waste tubes so they don't get blocked again, don't you? I mean, they're such a good team."

Chip went pale.

Lisa laughed, "Holy shit." Then covered her mouth.

"Exactly," Sin said, smiling.

"Oh, I think we can accommodate that," Gregory said. "I know there are people in my district who would appreciate their, uh, handling that, um, duty."

"No!" Chip said. "Anything but that!"

"Best offer I bet you're going to get, Chip," I offered, then more softly as he was escorted out of our apartment, "Though, your going out the airlock works for me…"

The Council vanished from the screen. Sin opened the panel beneath it and pulled the camera feed like Benny showed her before he left after repairing it.

"Well, how about that. We're still alive," I said.

Sin sighed, "For now, at least."

Lisa stared. "He's gone. Really out of my life?"

"You've nothing to worry about… He'll likely finding himself out the airlock without a suit, otherwise," Sin said.

Unable to help but shiver, Lisa sighed.

Moments later, Benny's wife returned with the pods with the sedated twins sleeping blissfully unaware of recent evidence. "Thank you so much," Sin said.

"We know who are friends are."

"As do we," I replied as she smiled and left.

"I hate having to medicate them like that," Sin said, checking on the babies in their pods.

"Let's hope we never have to again," I offered, lying back.

"Well, since they are sleeping, I need to deal with the repercussions of what we've just done."

I frowned. "Huh?"

Sin sighed, "You want to punish the spouses and children of Chip's people for what their foolish husbands did?"

Lisa's eyes widened. "They'll be saddled with years of Service."

"Unless something's done… not just for them, but for you, Lisa."

"Me?"

"You need to look at your stats. You've gotten credit for nursing Gary, but… Well, check your stats and talk until the kids wake and make that difficult."

Sin left as Lisa consulted the vid. "Oh…"

"Lisa?"

"They just changed my status from married to single."

"You mean, they're listed you as divorced?" horrified at the thought, knowing that our Charter specifically forbade it. We'd all signed on for "married until death do us part."

"No, they annulled my marriage… and I'm, uh, listed as an available surrogate."

"What?"

Lisa was awfully quiet as she came back over to me. "At least I won't have to pretend to be pregnant. I guess there are worse things…"

I met her gaze, "What?"

"I'm glad I'm not bearing his child… Perhaps, I can't at all."

"Lisa, you're still real young…"

She gave me a hard look. "I'm a woman… Colonial Management wouldn't have taken me, otherwise. You know that."

"Of course, you are," I answered. "You'll have children."

"But in the meantime, my debt to the Colony is being extended… I need to get pregnant and have kids…"

"Well, you will—in time."

She blinked, smiled. "As a surrogate."

"Sure."

"Oh, thank you, Gary!" she shouted, hugging me, the pressure on my still healing ribs making me see stars as I stared, confused. "You won't regret this! I'll carry your children—in, well, a, uh, few years so Sin won't have to!"

"Um, what?"

"Well, I could try sooner," she said, looking up at me, frowning.

"What?" I gasped. "That's not—" *what I meant at all.*

She blinked. Eyes going wide. "You mean, you'd want to father my children?"

My eyes must have gone wider than hers.

"Uh, I know you're married. I meant… you know, through insemination."

"Lisa," trying to break our hug, but she had my ribs in what felt like a death grip. "I think you and, um, Sin, need to have a long talk."

"We have."

"Err."

"While I was nursing you, we talked a lot. Especially about… lots of stuff."

I was horrified. "And that included, um, your being a surrogate."

"Of course, there's the Colonial Contract, and, well, the medbots say I should be able to carry to term."

I blinked, remembering to breathe.

"I'm just glad you understand," tears welling. "Because, because I'm never going to have Chip's babies!"

I nodded. "That, I can understand."

Tears beginning to stream down her cheeks, she pressed tighter, which didn't help my attempts to continue breathing. "Thank you… I was so afraid I might have to leave."

Wincing from the pain, "You're… you're not leaving. You're family, Lisa."

Her tears flowed. "I love you—" which is when she tilted her head up and pressed her lips to kiss me.

My eyes went wide. "Uh."

She blinked, "Um, I love you both."

I heard the hatch open, stared.

"Oh, good, you figured things out," Sin announced.

"Uh," I muttered, trying to look back at her past

Lisa, who thankfully let me go, leaving me to stagger. "You're back."

"As to that, Colonial Management, apparently, has their own plans…"

I heard an unfamiliar sound, then glimpsed it as Lisa whispered, "Oh."

"Who knew they had one of these?" Sin said, one of our bodyguards bringing in the pods behind it.

I stared at the unichair, which was basically a mechanized ball beneath an old style wheelchair-like frame.

"We going somewhere?" I asked.

Sin nodded. "You can say that…"

Chapter 12 – Moving Up in the World

Out of the apartment for the first time in weeks, you'd think I'd be excited. Fine, I didn't remember most of the injuries and my ribs, in particular, were killing me as I motored slowly down the corridor in my powered unichair. Sin carried our meager belongings besides me as Lisa pushed the barely stirring twins in their pods. Julio and his friends kept the gawkers back. I have to admit, I really appreciated Julio and his Fabricator gang. I suppose I should think of them as a team, but his, like a number of our teams, clearly were still of the streets.

I tried to ignore the somewhat disturbing looks of our curious neighbors as I wheeled forward, my left arm in a sling with the little model moon concealed within it, carrying my reader in my lap. My two most precious object possessions.

The young men and women, about half wearing their pressure suits as we were, peered at me, well, us, from their open hatchways, and began to wave and shout, "Grime!" almost as a cheer.

"Somehow, I don't think that's for me," Sin said.

I frowned.

"Definitely isn't," Lisa said, all too cheerily.

I chose to ignore that, though, as we followed the flashing light along the ceiling directing us to a dead end corridor, blocked by where I remembered a bulkhead style metal wall was. However, it wasn't a metal wall anymore. It had retracted, and now the wall was clearly something else.

"An elevator?" Lisa said, glancing at me.

Sin nodded, "In the message Colonial Management posted in the Commons listing us and the others… it did end with 'Enjoy the new digs.'"

As we waited several women with their gyropods rolling like baby buggies came up the corridor behind us, two of my bodyguards trailing behind them, "Boss? Good to see you. Have we really been promoted?"

"Apparently; and issued new quarters," I replied. "Wherever they are…" looking at Sin.

"You've got Benny promoted along with you…" Benny's wife, Ling, said to me.

"He was already Assistant Head Grubber," I replied.

"And I told him, you'd get him killed," Ling sighed, shaking her head, turning to stare at the elevator door.

"He still might," Sin replied, unhelpfully.

"He wouldn't tell me where you were sending him," Ling stated.

"You really don't want to know," I replied.

"But he'll definitely have deserved the promotion," Sin admitted.

I gave Sin a long look.

"You know I'm right."

Lisa choked back a laugh as Ling frowned.

"I'd have done it myself, if I could," I answered, knowing Benny deserved a lot more than a promotion for keeping me and my family safe.

The elevator doors opened.

I pressed my unichair's control and we entered. The doors closed as I swiveled the chair around. The floor trembled and we felt ourselves ascend for what felt longer than I could believe possible. When we came to a stop, a computer voice said, "Pressurization equilibrium check… Pressurization match. Doors opening."

"Oh, my," someone said as we gaped in what I realized was filtered sunlight.

"Where are we?" Lisa asked.

"Home, apparently," I said as Sin tapped my shoulder. I pressed the control, directing the chair forward into the expansive dome proceeding along the path. Trees— fruit bearing trees— lined the path, buildings visible in the distance and to the right and left.

"COLONIAL MANAGEMENT WELCOMES YOU. YOUR STATUS HAS BEEN UPGRADED BASED ON SKILLS, DECISION MAKING, AND DEMONTRATED APTITUDE OF FAMILY MEMBERS' CONCERNS OVER SELF-INTEREST FOR YOUR COLONY... EACH OF YOU, AND THOSE THAT WILL FOLLOW YOU IN THE COMING HOURS, ARE CHARGED WITH MAINTAINING THIS DOME, AND WILL HAVE DUTIES TO YOUR DISTRICT AND THE COLONY... YOU WILL BE ASSIGNED ADDITIONAL DUTIES BASED ON YOUR APTITUDES... PLEASE NOTE, FAILURE TO MEET EXPECTATIONS WILL RESULT IN YOUR FAMILY'S RETURN TO YOUR ORIGINATING DISTRICT APARTMENT."

I moved my unichair directly to the right, Sin and Lisa following as Ling and the others seemed dumbstruck. I drew up to the edge of the dome, which was made up of very familiar material.

Lisa gasped, "They've cut up hibernation pods."

"Nothing goes to waste, particularly the radiation shielding," I muttered, staring through the metal laced framing of the multiple paned, gas filled layers of the specially formatted glass. Beyond, there were arrays of solar panels—and incomplete domes amid a half dozen or so completed ones along the edge of the Valles Marneris canyon that stretched, literally, the equivalent of the length of the United States.

I frowned thinking I saw something, shaking my head, knowing it was impossible I swiveled my chair and glanced up.

"How many pods do you think they've cut up to make these domes?" Sin wondered.

"Colonies worth," I replied, figuring many of the

pods that brought us would meet a similar fate to the tens of thousands that made up just this dome, alone.

Lisa gaped, looking at the terraced scaffold like levels around the dome's perimeter, which I surmised helped with maintenance. "This dome is huge… How many people do you think can live here?"

"A lot more than the trainers who likely lived up here until they moved on," I mused.

The very wide center of the dome lay above a forest. Well, what I thought a forest must actually look like. Never having seen so many trees in one place before, except in pictures in the ecology database.

"Are those mirrors up there?" Sin wondered.

I frowned, squinting. I realized the sunlight did appear directed over a wide section of forest at the moment. "Must be. They could direct the light to best effect."

"And we really are going to live here?" Lisa muttered.

I nodded, "Apparently."

"Do… do you think we'll still need to wear these pressure suits all the time?"

"Lisa, I'm not sure we can trust the dome," Sin said. "Look at those domes out there… I don't think those there look that way because they weren't completed."

"That's a cheery thought," I muttered.

Sin shook her head, "We'll continue to wear these, whether we're advised to or not."

I sighed, agreeing, "Agreed, not trusting the integrity of the dome can't hurt."

We heard the twins stirring.

"Something else that won't hurt, is our checking out the schematics for this place," Sin said.

"Why do I think I've a lot more reading to do?" I smiled, my database and reader in my lap.

"Yeah, definitely a job for you," Sin said, taking

our now crying son out of his pod. Lisa knelt and brought out his fussy twin.

The babies grew quiet, blinking in the sunlight, so different from the artificial light they had known.

We headed back toward the elevator, doors closed, a red light flashing above it, before suddenly going dark, possibly indicating it had descended to pick up another group of promoted new residents. We could see Ling and the others further up the paths splitting up through the trees following different colored lit lines.

"PLEASE PROCEED ALONG THE GREEN LIT PATH," a recorded voice announced, the green lights built into the path blinked, insistent. We followed it into the trees, my eyes misting at the realization that even the trees had had to leave Earth to survive.

Lisa swallowed hard, the babies settled back in their pods, staring at the leaves and branches as I motored along the path as we crossed the dome. We were led over a stone bridge with a little brook passing beneath it.

"This is like out of a storybook," Sin muttered.

I chuckled, "You actually had a storybook as a kid?"

"I know," Sin admitted, "we were lucky to even have one."

We paused on the bridge and listened to the water traveling down the brook, feeling the gentle breeze. "It's beautiful," Lisa whispered.

I turned my chair around and couldn't disagree. "Welcome to Mars."

Sin glanced at me and actually smiled.

I pushed the control and continued following the green flashing lights. We passed a tented structure that had its own pressurized hatches. We paused to check it out, glancing through the misted translucent material that made up the walls. "What is it?" Lisa asked.

"A greenhouse," I surmised.

"Well, we won't go hungry," Sin offered.

I gave her a look before turning the chair to return to the path through the trees. When we came out of the forest, we found ourselves facing rectangular two-story structures, windows only at the upper level. The fabricated buildings were built close to the descending curve of the outer dome. There was a familiar looking pressured hatch at the entrance.

"Well, they aren't completely trusting," I commented as the blinking green lights of the path led directly up to the hatch which cycled open, invitingly, with the sound of suddenly released air.

"Welcome home," I said, gesturing with my good arm.

"No picket fence," Sin chuckled.

"Um," Lisa said, hesitating. "I was really on the list with you?"

Sin smiled, "Yes, you really were. Now, come on, let's check out our new place."

I motored forward and we entered the lock, which cycled, opening to a corridor.

A monitor screen lowered from the ceiling and lit up. "Welcome, Mr. and Mrs. Grime—and Miss Lisa."

Chapter 13 – Mars Isn't Just a Harsh Master

"Sarge," I said, waving to the familiar face on the vid.

"Grime, I see you have managed to keep your sense of humor… Oh, and congratulations on not having gotten yourself killed yet. This is the largest townhouse under the dome, so do your best not to get lost."

I shook my head, "We'll do that, Sarge."

Sin was staring around us, likely thinking what I fleetingly had; that this place was big enough for four families, if not more.

"You've likely noticed, you've two floors. You've an elevator to six lower levels. Bad news is you only have access to two of them at your present clearance levels. Good news is you now have a med bay, which will help speed your healing.

"And, you've a comm center allowing you access to the Grubber District and work area—and Central. You're officially Grubber Management after you transition the Head Grubber position as you choose."

"That'll be Benny."

"Thought so. Now, about those Fabricator gang members—"

"I'll be promoting Julio and his team. They'll definitely enjoy handling sonic regulators over fabricating."

"Giving those to gang members might not be the smartest thing, Grime."

"Well, as I see it, we're going to need all the help we can get to run this place. It's huge…And, we've only so many people from my Grubber Team to count on."

"I think I know some we can recruit," Sin said with a smile.

"Our projections still shows this Colony's survival only at thirty-four percent."

"What was it yesterday?"

Sarge paused, chuckled, "Eleven."

"Well, I'm sure we, and the people you've promoted to the other domes will change that."

Sighing, "Grime, no other district has anyone being promoted… None normally would be for weeks, if not months. And, you need to get the Grubbers to repair the damage from that accident that nearly killed you. The teams haven't gone back since. You need to get them back to schedule… We need those areas completed for expansion as much as we need the fertilizer production back on track."

I nodded, "For the next bunch of immigrants?"

"We plan ahead, Grime… No resources can ever be allowed to go to waste—and new colonists are real useful. We'll use new immigrants for as long as they survive. I know it's rather Darwinian, but, believe me, letting anyone your age thinks this is school where you might just get a bad grade gets people killed in lots."

At my look, Sarge said, "Sorry, I forgot, your people offer you High School only on the Net… Well, let's just say our method best promotes the advancement of civilization and terraforming, well, Mars-a-forming of this planet."

Sin set her right hand on my shoulder, "No pressure, Gary."

"Oh, not just on him, Mrs. Grime," Sarge responded.

Sin frowned. "Sir?"

"You'll be reporting to me, too, Mrs. Grime, and will be meeting with your new lady friends regularly at their place. I suggest you have a chat with your district and conceal the fact anyone's been promoted for the time being…"

"In that case," Sin said ever so matter-of-factly, "could you arrange for the team widows and their children to be sent here?"

I glanced at her as Sarge frowned, "Why?"

"Well, while Gary was unconscious, I met with them—"

"We know… and were disappointed at their refusal to remarry any of the widowers in your District."

"Um, under the circumstances it didn't seem the proper thing to do."

"You all need to take your contractual obligations rather seriously, Mrs. Grime."

"I know… They know, too—and they're willing to surrogate or remarry someday. But in the meantime, since they, and the other families of Gary's team, have been helping each other out, it seems their, uh, situation could be put to better advantage, um, here under the dome."

"And you figure Service here will provide them better credit?" he asked, less than trustingly.

"Why, of course," Sin replied.

"Fine, I'll see to it."

I looked from one to the other. "Sarge, that was too easy. What are you up to?" I asked.

Sarge sighed. "Foolish or unlucky colonists do not live long, Grime… Those who play things in ways we think offer your colony better chances, such as the Missus' suggestion, well, let's say, we're willing try to help a bit."

I glanced down at the object in my sling, the little Deimos with the remote once more hidden inside it.

"But, we have our limits, Grime. That you asked for leniency for your murderous rival was viewed as foolish by many, but to Colonial Management's computer, it looked at things differently—as I said, that jump in those projections was remarkable."

"So, Sarge, you're still officially not talking to Colony Central."

"The Colony is officially on its own, Grime. People

are going to die… That's how it is. Understand that. Lots of people are going to die here. You need to help as many survive as possible to create a sustainable and viable colony. Do what needs doing, no matter that many of you are rather young for the responsibility.

"But I warn you, Mars is a harsh master… the ultimate disciplinarian. Don't think for a moment that life's going to get any easier—widowed neighbors or those you trust around you or not. You all owe a great deal of Service against your passage and maintenance here—and living in the dome, well, doubles your Service debt."

I sighed as Lisa gasped, staring at us. Sin didn't seem surprised in the least. I held up Deimos, "Thanks for this, Sarge."

"Grime, don't thank me; and keep my present close, you'll doubtless need it again… but it won't help protect you from someone smacking you over the head with an even bigger rock."

"Well, I'll just have to make myself a slingshot for this, then—the low g will make it pretty effective."

"If you don't miss," Sarge offered.

Sin glanced at me and shook her head. "He does tend to aim high."

I sighed, "Sarge, how can I thank you—we thank you?"

Sarge nodded, "Don't thank me, Kid. If and when your colony proves it can sustain itself and more people survive than the just over two hundred did of my own colony—that will be thanks enough."

With that the vid image went dark.

"Shit," I muttered as Lisa looked horrified.

"Two hundred?" Sin repeated.

The vid changed to a display—an all too familiar display. Each of us saw our stats on the split screen. Lisa's name had the word "surrogate to the Grime family, pending," flashing.

"Somehow," I admitted, "I don't think I'll be able to turn off the cameras this time."

"No, and we do seem rather surrounded by vids," Sin said, glancing about, then saw the playpen and the cradles in the living room off to the right. "Well, those look nice, at least."

"Well, we're home, ladies," I grinned.

We explored the rooms of the first floor as Sin settled the kids down in the pen.

"We've a full kitchen," Lisa called out, sounding delighted.

I glimpsed her looking through the inset cupboard, "And we're fully stocked with packet meals… And, and we've—we've noodles and sauces, too!"

"Well, this is going to be interesting," Sin said, peering into one of the other rooms. "We've a weight room, which will help with your rehab."

I motored the unichair and entered the room, "Kid sized equipment, too… Though, it'll be years before they'll be ready for it."

"I'm not sure how safe this area will be for inquisitive little hands. We'll need to keep this room closed, whether we're working in here or not."

I directed my chair back out of the room and across the main level, pausing before an elevator door, a spiral staircase next to it on the left.

The elevator door opened and I maneuvered my chair inside, then tapped the pad for the upper floor. The elevator door closed and up it went delivering me to the upper level. I explored, finding a vid in each room, rooms as big as our former apartment, a number significantly larger. All offered retractable furniture, except the room I knew had to be the nursery. I suppose any of the others we didn't need as bedrooms could be used as playrooms or a study. I made my way just halfway across the upper level, when I found the master bedroom.

I motored across the room with its large bed, pausing before the inner plexi of the wall length hatch to the wide balcony beyond, which I was half afraid was really a wall vid image. I set my reader and little Deimos on a small table before going to the balcony's access pad.

Keying it, the inner plexi retracted into the walls on the right and left. I motored in and the hatch cycled closed behind me. The panel soon flashed "pressure equalized" before the plexi slid aside to the balcony.

I went onto the deck, feeling the breeze, and took in the view of the landscape and through the dome out at the distant canyon's side edge and looked hard for what I thought I'd seen earlier.

Chapter 14 – Mars is the God of War of Wills

Frowning, I heard the hatch cycle and Sin came up behind me. "I decided to bring the twins up. Lisa's changing them."

Turning the chair, nodding, I took a deep breath, "Uh, good of her."

"She's better with them than I am," Sin admitted.

I hesitated, suddenly at a loss for words, "Quite a view we have here."

"Gary, quite a place we have here. You've done better for us than I had any right to expect when we agreed to marry."

I turned the chair about and met her gaze. "I know I'll never be able to give you the world, but I can, at least, offer you a great view."

She put her hand on my shoulder and with the other turned my chair back about. "Mars is beautiful in its own way, isn't it?"

"And it'll do everything it can to kill us," I replied.

"There is that," she sighed.

"They say there was water here once until the core cooled. Looking at that canyon, I believe it. The Grand Canyon got nothing on it."

"You would think Mars would want life to return."

"I think we're going to have to claw for it."

"What else is new?" Sin sighed.

"There's that, but…"

"Mars," she replied, "is not going to kill us, Gary… We survived Earth. We made it during the crossing through space and survived hibernation. We will survive this place."

I sighed, glancing at my sling and legs. "Mars didn't do this to me, Sin."

"Gary, please don't say that in Lisa's hearing. She needs to look ahead, know there's hope for us—and needs all the love we can give her for that matter. She's had more than enough of the other."

"Believe me, I understand that."

"No, I'm not sure you do, Gary." She faced me. "She's half in love with you."

"I've no intention of messing with her—"

"I know. But she may welcome it, not realizing, no matter what our Colonial contract says that she's not ready for, well, motherhood." She shook her head, "I certainly am not. I—fear for our babies all the time. Though, I may not show it."

"Sin, I—worry for them, you, even Lisa all the time, too. She's just a kid… You can see that."

"By law and our Charter we're not, and she's not. She'll be expected to meet those damned contractual obligations all too soon," Sin said, meeting my gaze. "Truth be told, she needs our help to heal from bruises on the inside, not just the ones we can see."

"We've an entire colony made up of broken people—just like us, if they didn't have it worse."

"I know," her gaze suddenly distant, tinged with defiance.

"That why we came here, Sin. It's not like we had anyplace else to go."

"Gary I've come to think Lisa would have been better off if Colonial Management had matched her with you... and not me."

"Don't say that."

"Gary, I don't deserve you. Believe me, I really don't."

I waved my arm in the sling, "I don't deserve you. I'm a nobody—and now, literally, a broken man. I can't even be much help with the kids… I'm just a guy with a clearance and, apparently, some luck."

We cycled back into the bedroom, the plexi to the balcony sealing behind us. "PRESURIZATION COMPLETE."

"Gary, you were never a nobody," Sin said, meeting my gaze as the inner plexi wall retracted. "Though, I admit, I thought so the moment I saw you… Now that we're here, we can fix you up. Though, even if we couldn't, you're smart, certainly not lucky to end up this way, but you do have a good heart. Which is why I'm rather fond of you, and also why Lisa saved your life and why she clearly intends to continue hanging around and, well, help out." She tussled my hair. "One thing I'm sure of, though, in that chair or out of it, I'm pretty sure Mars has met its match."

"Sin, Mars has met it match in us."

"Well," she looked over her shoulder, "you and I both know we're not likely to reach old age…"

"We certainly weren't going to back home."

She nodded, "We need to do everything we can to see that's not true for the kids or the rest of our first generation Martians."

"Sin, you know…"

"I know there's a good chance none of us will make it, but let me make one thing clear—" She leaned over, pressing her lips to mine.

My eyes went wide as she took my breath away, "Um. Hmm."

"I'm your wife, and you are my husband—until death do us part… Now, I'm going to check on the twins, then I want to see if your clearance is good enough to get me to that medbay. You need to start cell regen therapy if we're to ever get you up and walking again."

"So, you read about the downside of injuries in micro and low gravity."

"Of course, I did. Lisa and I had plenty of time to read that section of the medical database… The bone loss you're sustaining can't be countered without significant time in a medbay, and Colonial Management generally isn't known for investing in healing colonists.

I guess, unless they're living in these domes, of course. I just wish there was more Lisa and I could have done for you."

"You two haven't done badly." I frowned. "But I can't say I'm looking forward to being immobilized in a regen pod…"

"We have a valuable resource—but for all we know there's an entire medbay level here, somewhere."

"Which could help everyone."

"Yeah," Sin said, looking thoughtful.

Frowning, "I know that look, Sin. What are you thinking?"

She frowned, glancing away, when Lisa rushed to the bedroom doorway, grinning, hair dripping wet, pressure suit pulled down off her shoulders, "I've the kids in a playpen I found—and I found a shower—a real shower and a bathtub, well, it's more of a small pool! I've got it filling with hot water! Sin, uh, would you mind watching the kids now?"

"Go!" Sin chuckled as Lisa ran off, shouting, "Better not use up all the hot water!"

"I won't!" Lisa yelled back.

"Gary, looks like we'll be able to clean up real nice, so we won't mess up those clean sheets or mess up the medbay."

I leaned back, glanced at the mattress, thicker than the folded piece of foam I knew all too well, and shook my head.

"Well, loverboy, don't be getting any ideas about getting lucky any time soon," she said, briefly pausing just beyond the doorway.

"Me? As brittle as I am?"

Sin looked at me. "Somehow, I think you wouldn't mind me breaking you into little pieces."

I grinned crookedly. "Some things are worth it."

We could hear the babies beginning to cry.

"That's my call," Sin said, leaving me staring after

her.

I heard a splash and Lisa shout down the hall, "Oh, yeah!"

I sighed, turning my chair to face the vid in the room. "Vid on," I said. "Schematic of this dome."

A map of the dome appeared with what had to be more than thirty townhouses. Then there were the ten greenhouses. The vid split screened, showing people arriving at the dome and Benny's wife and kids settling in to their place. The others, well, um, settling in. Then an image of me looking at the vid appeared in its place; Sin now in a robe in the next room breast feeding. Another view opening, focusing on Lisa in the small pool delightedly soaping herself.

I smiled, then realized I shouldn't be watching her, particularly when Sin looked uncannily right back at me on the screen. Then the screen expanded to focus solely on Lisa in the pool, making her big as life.

"Vid, cut the feed to the bathroom!"

"UNABLE TO COMPLY."

My eyes widening, "Block that feed."

"UNABLE TO COMPLY."

"Override. Shunt view to the landscape!"

"ACKNOWLEDGED."

"Who was controlling that?" I asked, staring at a satellite view of the canyon system, dotted with clusters of domes.

The computer made no answer.

I sat back in the unichair. The vid suddenly filled with an image of me sitting here. Grimacing, I stared back, understanding the message from Colonial Management.

Whether on Earth or Mars they wanted me to know there was nothing we could really hide. What more that message conveyed, well, that didn't bear thinking about. But in that moment, seeing myself in the unichair, arm and legs splinted, I felt a chilling fear that this was one challenge I couldn't beat.

How long I sat there staring at my reflection on the screen, I don't know.

"Gary?"

I glanced to the doorway and there Lisa was wrapped in a towel. "Gary, you all right?"

"You should still be in the bath."

She shook her head, "I had this funny feeling—I guess it was the idea I might be wasting all that hot water."

"Well, Sin will appreciate that," I said, knowing it sounded lame.

"You look rather serious, Gary."

"It's nothing," I said, the thought of them watching her, making me spy on her in that moment, knowing they were watching all of us. I sat up straighter and smiled, knowing she deserved none of this. "I hope you enjoyed the bath."

"It was wonderful," she grinned. "How about that shower?"

I glanced back at the vid, now dark. "Perhaps later."

She frowned, "Gary, you look so serious."

"Sorry, I guess being here is hitting me."

She glanced down at herself, "Is… is my being here making you uncomfortable?"

Shaking my head, "No, I'm happy you're here. I'm just worried about our family."

"Our… our family?"

I nodded, "Our family, Lisa."

She eyes widening. "You mean that."

"Of course, I do. You're part of this family, Lisa."

Tears misting, she nodded, "I feel that way, too…"

"You've saved my life… and trusted us with yours."

She choked up a bit, wiping sudden tears, "Oh, I'm being so silly." She rushed up to me and threw her arms around me. She kissed my cheek, making me blush.

"Um, Lisa."

She let me go and hastily stood back. "You really stink. I'm giving you a sponge bath, at least."

Before I could argue she rushed from the room. I blinked, knowing I'd not be able to peel down the top of my pressure suit without help.

"Lean forward," Lisa said, sponging my back, the tepid water cold against my skin.

Sin paused in the doorway, wearing the robe she'd found. "He's smells better already."

"Why, thanks," I said as she came in and tossed two robes on the bed.

"Thanks," Lisa then grinned. "We're now really Martians, aren't we?" settling her right hand on my shoulder, glancing out through the plexi at the dome beyond the balcony.

"Of course, we are," I said, feeling whole, no matter that my body was broken.

"Gary, you're crying," Sin said. "You all right? Perhaps, we should get you down to the medbay right now."

"What? No, I'm fine," I said. "It's just," I wiped the unconscious tears from my cheeks, "we're home, aren't we? Really home."

Lisa wrapped her arms around me from behind, "Of course, we are—nowhere safer."

Sin met my gaze.

"We'll make it even safer, that I promise," I said. Lisa moved and began to dry my back.

"Lisa, I'd best take him to the medbay. Watch the twins, please—so Gary can keep that promise to stand on his own two feet."

Helping me put on the robe, Lisa asked, "Want me to prepare dinner?"

"Would you?" Sin said. "That would be

wonderful."

Lisa nodded, donning the robe, letting her towel drop to the floor.

"Sin, can you help me pull up my pressure suit?"

"Let's leave you as you are for now… It'll make it easier getting you into the medbay later."

"I can put it and ours in the sonic I saw downstairs," Lisa offered as she left us.

Sin nodded as I turned the damp seated unichair. Drawing her robe tighter, she met my gaze.

"Someone's messing with us," I whispered.

She leaned close, whispered back, "I know," kissing me.

I met her gaze as she drew back.

"Medbay after dinner," she suggested.

"It's going to hurt."

She nodded, "A lot."

I sighed. "Sin, mind going back on the balcony with me for a moment?"

"Only a moment… You feel safe without our being covered up in our pressure suits?"

"We'll only be out a few minutes, tops." I turned my chair around. Sin activated the door. We cycled our way through.

"You really do like the view," she smiled, feeling the breeze.

"Uh, I need you to look, uh, that way."

"Huh, why?"

"Please, I need to know if I'm crazy or not." She gave me a look. I pointed, "Down there. Tell me you see what I do."

Going up to the balcony railing, she peered across the canyon, which stretched for miles, glancing at the terrain so far below, then her eyes widened. "What?" Gasped, "What the—"

"It has to be a trick of the light," I muttered.

There was what looked like the outline of giant

arm and hand holding a torch in the stretch of terrain.

"Well," Sin says, "I do feel suddenly welcome on Mars," Sin sighed as I brought up my chair next to her as we stared, neither of us caring if it was real, a trick of gazing through the dome, or just a play of shadows, feeling an inexplicable sense of wonder… and hope.

About the Author

D. H. Aire has always been interested in the past and future. Wondering about his family' past, he researched his family's immigration experience over the years and learned a great deal about Ellis Island and what it was like for his great-grandparents and grandparents, who came with only a few dollars in their pockets to the United States with nowhere else to go. Starting new lives in America, they struggled to succeed against what must have felt like impossible odds. For me, I imagine that's a universal experience and could well be the immigrant experience on Mars one day. That is the genesis of this story, which is essentially a reverse Ellis Island experience, taking America's huddled masses and leaving for literally a new world.

In addition to writing science fiction, D.H. writes epic fantasy with a twist, which has found expression in his writing of his *Highmage's Plight Series* and *The Hands of the Highmage Series,* and the more contemporary *Dare2Believe* series. He is also the author of the space opera series, *Terran Catalyst.* Additionally, his short stories have appeared in ezines and anthologies.

D.H. Aire is originally from St. Louis, Missouri and currently resides in the Washington, D.C. metropolitan area. To learn more about *Nowhere to Go But Mars* and his other projects, visit the author's website, www.dhaire.net or follow him on Twitter at @DHAire15 or Dare 2 Believe on Facebook.

* 9 7 9 8 6 0 5 2 2 3 4 5 0 *

Gary Grime knows the odds are against him. He like millions of others his age have no hope of opportunity – not unless they're healthy enough to possibly survive the equivalent of steerage class in hibernation for the one-way trip to Mars.

He's literally nowhere else to go. And, if he reaches the planet, the odds of survival grow worse, not better for him and the thousands making the trip.

Grime like the rest of Americas huddled young masses have an opportunity for a new life, one they will need to build on a new world, well, beneath its uninhabitable surface.

Who knew how apt naming a planet for the God of War could be? Or that not everything is quite what it seems. Gary's no fool, but is he prepared – are any of the colonial hopefuls prepared for what's in store for them?

Welcome to D.H. Aire's novella, *Nowhere to Go But Mars.*

Laboratory Manual on Biochemistry and Biotechnology

Krishanu, Shweta & Shailendra